A VIKING GHOST FOR VALENTINE'S DAY

JO-ANN CARSON

2016 Jo-Ann Carson Terpstra

JRT Publications

ISBN 978-1-989031-11-7

Cover Art by Steven Novak

❄ Created with Vellum

INTRODUCTION

To feed her three children, Widow Abigail Jenkins takes the only job available in Sunset Cove: night cleaner in the notorious, haunted teahouse. She figures the wild, supernatural rumors about the place are pure fiction. After all, ghosts don't exist.

Eric Eklund, a sexy spirit from Sweden, is over a thousand years old. Having missed his chance at Valhalla, the Viking spends his time roaming the world and gambling. That is, until he sees Abby whose feisty, earthly-spirit turns his ghostly world upside down.

When the two meet sparks fly, but their romance is interrupted by a poltergeist hunting children.

What happens when you mix a naughty Viking ghost, built like a Norse god, a strong woman who suffers no fools and a nasty poltergeist? Answer: another fun Gambling Ghost story.

A *Viking Ghost for Valentine's Day* is a lighthearted novella filled with love, laughter and just enough ghouliness to thrill and chill you to the bone.

"The boundaries which divide Life from Death are at best shadowy and vague. Who shall say where the one ends, and where the other begins." Edgar Allan Poe

PREFACE

THE REVIEWERS LOVE THIS BOOK

Over 45 Reviews on Amazon (4.5 stars)

Fun, scary, and funny

This is the delightful novella that started Mrs. Carson's. "Abby and Eric" series about a widowed mother janitor/detective and her ghostly boyfriend. The series continues with "Midnight Magic" (a full-length novel), and "I Messed up Christmas" (another novella). This is a quick and entertaining read, with numerous descriptive touches that capture the "spirit" of ghost stories. Jo-Ann Carson is a talented writer with delightful wit and a fine feel for plot. I first read "Midnight Magic" in late 2017, and Mrs. Carson immediately moved into the upper tier of my favorite authors.

5 Star Amazon Review By <u>Brent Butler</u>TOP 1000 REVIEWER

*****

Loving these ghosts! Sweet and romantic. Makes you want your own "haunted" house.

5 Star Amazon review by Marianne

*****

A warm mystery cozy set in the Pacific Northwest? Sign me up! Abby, a tired, but compassionate mother of three, who'd do anything to support her childern, including taking janitorial work at a haunted tea house, meets a handsome Scandinavian man with a manly-man scent of wood smoke and a sexy voice. The only problem? He's a viking ghost! For a fast, short romp of a story, Jo-Ann Carson packs a lot of humour, mystery and adventure into her romantic tale. I definitely recommend this short story.

5 star Amazon review by JT
*****

A Wonderful Warm Loving story. No sex but you will not miss it. It makes you want your own consider ghost. I loved the story.

5 star Amazon review by Kindle Customer
*****

CHAPTER 1

THE HAUNTED TEAHOUSE

Abigail Jenkins stood with her hands on her hips in the pouring rain, staring at the famous teahouse across the street, the one with the wicked reputation for all things supernatural. She expected it to shimmer, or gurgle, or do something odd at any moment, but the structure did nothing of the sort. It was a tired, old house in need of paint and repair, on a street of tired, old houses. Its cloak of normalcy seduced her, daring her to come closer for a better look, as if it were a witch in a pretty dress offering poisoned candy, but she had heard the wicked stories about the place and she was no fool. Things happened in this house, things that were far from ordinary. A shiver slithered up her spine. *Of all the haunted houses in all the world, why did this one pick me?*

Trying to shake off a sense of foreboding as thick as molasses, she wiped the rain off her face and crossed the street to face the house. Whether she liked it or not, the only job available in Sunset Cove was night cleaner in this place and she needed a job.

Being a widow with three kids to feed, the word "choice" had vanished from her vocabulary a long time ago. The place could be haunted by the devil himself and it still wouldn't matter. She needed money, especially now her baby was sick and needed expensive meds. Gulping down the paralyzing fear brewing in her blood she climbed the long, wooden staircase to the front door. It opened before she knocked.

"Good evening." The woman standing on the threshold looked over a pair of tortoise-shell reading glasses, perched precariously on her long, narrow nose. Around her neck she wore a large agate pendant. Abby couldn't place the woman's exotic accent, but her voice sounded human.

"Hi, I'm Abigail Jenkins. You can call me Abby." She reached out her hand. "I'm here to see about the cleaning job listed on Findit.com."

The woman opened the door wide and motioned with her head for Abby to enter. "You're new in town?" Her eyes roved over Abby.

"Yes. I've been here a week."

"And you want the cleaning job."

"Yes." Hadn't she just said that? Abby wondered what other jobs the woman had listed in the local on-line swap-and-shop site. She smiled and hoped she looked like a good candidate. It felt good to get out of the cold February rain, and so far, she had survived her first contact in the house. Looking around she could see no murderers, no vampires …

"We don't have vampires," the woman said, as if she read her thoughts. "I imagine they smell bloody awful. My name is Azalea and this is my teahouse."

Abby nodded. Had the older woman read her mind?

"Yes," she said, leaning closer. "I do read minds, when I choose to. But I don't bite." A smile tugged at the corner of her mouth.

"That must get you into trouble."

"Sometimes it does." The woman's hazel eyes softened. "I read tea leaves for a living." She pointed to the large, open area beside where she stood. "This is our reception room."

Two soft sofas, assorted wing chairs and small tables covered with magazines filled the space nicely. The color scheme was a muted rose with darker rose accents. Lacy curtains circa the 1800s covered the windows. It had a frozen-in-time feel. A picture of it would fit nicely on the cover of a *Better Homes and Gardens for Ghosts and Ghouls* ezine.

Azalea's chin rose as if she didn't approve of Abby's thought. "You need to vacuum and straighten this area every night. It gets a lot of traffic. Now follow me and I'll show you the rest of the house."

Abby shook off the feeling of being slowly swallowed up by the place as she followed the woman into the first room to their right.

"I call this Agatha's room after my mother who was named after the great Agatha Christie. Most of my customers come here, so it gets the dirtiest and will need the most attention. People drop a lot of crumbs." She stopped and exhaled noisily. "Will you stop thinking about your baby?"

Abby swallowed and nodded.

"I want the floor swept and spot cleaned nightly. Once a week it should be disinfected. We don't want to be spreading germs. All table surfaces must be …"

Abby made mental notes of her duties. Later she would create a check list for herself on her computer, before she got back to her writing.

Azalea raised a threaded brow. "Yes, a list would be good. I'd like to see it when you're done. I might need to add something to it. Writing?"

So much for having any thoughts for yourself. "I ... I write stories."

"Love stories? I hope so. The world needs more of those."

"Mystery, actually,"

Her nose lifted. "Let's move to the second tea room."

It looked much like the first. Faded floral wallpaper, old furniture and a creaky wooden floor. But this one had a cat, a sleek black cat. It lifted its head for a second, looked straight at her as if it were checking her out and closed its eyes. Okay, that was creepy, but the haunted house ambience was so strong, it felt overdone, kitschy.

"This is Lilith's room. I use it for special readings." Azalea tilted her head until the white hair piled on top threatened to spill over. "And that"—she pointed to the cat sitting in the window seat,— "is Lilith." The cat meowed softly.

Abby nodded and followed her back into the hallway. They walked past a closed door, about which Azalea said nothing, and on to a large kitchen area at the back. "I expect Rita the cook will keep this area clean, but I would like you to look it over every night to make sure the stove and burners are off and no food has been left out for the mice." She grimaced.

"You can make yourself coffee or tea here. The washrooms to the left need nightly cleaning as well. The door beside them leads to the basement, but you don't need to bother with that." She pointed towards the far wall. "The back door leads to a porch and stairs. There's an alley that runs behind the house."

Abby nodded. "Is that it?"

"Yes. It will be hard work, but you look like you're up to it. You can start tonight. I'll pay you twenty dollars an hour for three hours and your first check will be on Friday. But, let me be clear: I expect to see three hours of work completed when I return every morning. I'll keep an extra chores list on the fridge, so if you finish your regular work early, you can attend to one of them."

Abby nodded. It sounded like a workable plan.

"Occasionally I will ask you to decorate. Valentine's Day is coming soon, and I like to have my teahouse reflect the love of the season. I'll bring a box of decorations up from the basement soon." She paused and wiggled her nose.

Abby sniffed. There was a different smell in this room, but it was a kitchen after all.

Azalea looked intently at her, as if she was considering what else to say. "When you take a break, help yourself to our house tea and coffee." She pointed to the canisters on the counter. "There are tea balls in the drawer, and cups and pots in the cupboard. Just remember to clean up after yourself."

"Thank you."

"I think that's all. You can make your own hours between 6 p.m. and 6 a.m. Come and go as you please, as long as you put in three hours of cleaning."

Abby smiled. This job was sounding better by the minute. Good pay and flexible hours would make life a lot easier for her. And the boss seemed all right, sort of, in an odd but not unkindly way.

"Do you have any questions?" Azalea tucked a loose strand of white hair back into her bun."

"What about the other room?"

Azalea looked around her, as if she were looking for a stray puppy. "What other room?"

"The third door on the right from the entrance."

"Oh, that one." She arched a brow. "You don't have to worry about it."

"If I get the other rooms done in time, and I think I will, I could at least sweep it out for you." Abby was sucking-up and she knew it. Doing extra impressed employers and she needed this job. She would do anything to keep her new boss happy.

"No."

No? Abby's curiosity piqued. "Are you sure?"

"Let me be clear. You are *not* to clean the third room."

"But—"

"Under *no* circumstances are you to go into that room."

"But—"

"Don't open *that* door."

"I see."

"No, I don't think you do. You must not, I repeat, you must not go into that room. No matter what you hear, or smell, or feel, you must not go into that room."

Abby raised her hand as if she were pledging an oath. "Ms. Azalea. I need this job. I promise I will do the best I can at every task you give me, and I won't go into the third room." *But I sure want to.*

The older woman exhaled loudly, and a shadow crossed her stormy gray eyes. "Good." She handed Abby a set of keys. "Let me show you the janitor's cupboard."

~

The winter storm grew stronger at dinner time, just as she was feeding the kids their last package of noodles. New to life on the west coast, the sound of the howling wind unsettled her. It felt sinister and dangerous. She knew it was only wind, but its roar spoke directly to her bones and bypassed her brain completely.

If I'm to live here, I'm going to have to get used to this. She walked over to the front window and watched the weather system transform their neighborhood. Trees groaned under the strain of the wind, branches broke and fell to the ground, cluttering the sidewalks and street. Rain pelted down from the sk, forming rivers on the roadway. Nature's wrath felt both exhilarating and terrifying.

But the storm didn't keep Abby's mind off her sick baby for long. As she watched the giant cedar trees sway, she said a silent prayer for Jane; that she would get better, that the medication would kick-in soon and work its magic.

~

*A*bby returned to the teahouse at eleven that night in the thick of the storm. Having had the grand tour, she told herself the place would feel less threatening than it had on first sight, but, once inside, its ominous presence gave her the chills. *No one ever died of the chills.* She set about her work.

A stubborn layer of dirt covered the hardwood floor of the reception area and turned out to be trickier to remove than she had anticipated, but once she got on her hands and knees and scrubbed one small section at a time, she got through it. Azalea's old vacuum cleaned the oriental rug easily and left it looking fluffy. After wiping down the coffee tables and straightening the magazines, she stood for a moment to assess her progress. The reception area looked good, in a Best Kept Haunted Houses kind of way.

For the first time in a long time, Abby took a deep breath. She had a job she could do and she was rocking it. Good things do come to those willing to work hard.

With the same attention to detail, she cleaned the Agatha tea room until it shone.

Next came Lilith's domain. A prickly sensation danced along her arms as she entered. The air was cooler. Lilith lifted her eyes to take Abby in and then plunked her head down again.

"Nice kitty. Good kitty," Abby said edging closer to her.

Normally she would have no reservations about approaching a cat. She liked cats. But something about this one, made her more than a little hesitant. She made a mental note to bring cat treats the following night. Carefully she reached her hand out to pet her, but the cat hissed and she pulled her hand back.

Outside the southeaster howled. Through the single-paned windows of the old house, she could hear the wind gusting off the ocean. Rain drummed on the roof and the wooden siding. She laughed out loud. It was a dark and stormy night.

Just before midnight she headed for the kitchen to make herself a cup of tea. As she passed the third door on the right, the forbidden door, she heard a sound and froze.

The house was supposed to be empty, but something was scraping along the wooden floor. It sounded like chairs. She swallowed. Then came muffled voices and laughter. Laughter in an empty room, at midnight? The tiny hairs on the back of her neck stood on end, but she straightened her shoulders, determined to take on whatever crap the universe decided to throw her way. It couldn't be spirits. *Ghosts don't use chairs.*

She sniffed. *Is that cigar smoke?*

Abby stood outside the third door shaking her head. The sounds and the smell were distinct. Someone was in that room. But she needed this job. And she couldn't look. Not if she wanted to keep her janitor position. *Oh fudge!* Her fingers itched to touch the door handle. If she could just peek, she could set aside her crazy fears. Azalea would never know. She reached out and stopped before she touched the delicate glass knob. Abby always kept her word.

So what could she do?

Live with it. She would have to live with the out-of-place noises and that horrible cigar stench. No one ever died from such things. She pulled out her phone and turned on her radio app. Country music blared, drowning out the third-room sounds. But her body knew they were still there. A woman screamed and Abby's gut clenched. *I can't go in there.* She sang along with her music, trying to drown the fear that bubbled within her.

I'm not alone.

CHAPTER 2

DEALT A WILD CARD

Swedish ghost Eric Eklund approached the teahouse for a game of poker. The downpour gave the scene a wonderfully ghoulish atmosphere that made him feel at home. He had been the grand-loser of a poker game last week, and had to accept the ultimate loss: two nights haunting Stevens, the local politician who wanted to close the town's one and only casino. Although Eric had thought it would be a boring, ghostly exercise, it had turned out to be fun. The guy got so scared he dropped his cell phone in the bath tub. He so deserved to be razzed. The idiot was going all-righteous on the town people and telling them gambling would ruin their lives and their community, as if it were a deadly virus. Pompous ass. Eric smiled at the memory of the terror in the politician's face when Eric helped him shave and then used his shaving cream to write a message on the mirror. "Support gambling."

Normally Eric entered the poker room directly through the window. His friend Rufus, who owned the house when he was alive, preferred to keep the game as private as possible, because his sister Azalea ran a tea-leaf reading business in the other rooms. Live humans came and went regularly, usually in the daytime, but occasionally by appointment at night. She had nothing against ghosts, but she didn't want Rufus and his friends scaring her customers. This made little sense. The people who came for a psychic reading must believe, at least a little, that spirits and other dimensions exist or they wouldn't be asking for their fortune's to be read, and if that were the case why the hell should they care about a bunch of ghosts playing cards in the next room? But Eric didn't bother Rufus with his opinion.

People didn't bother Rufus period. Once the ruthless leader of the Black Angels biker gang, he now held court with a number of badass spirits. Seriously badass.

But his poker games rocked. Ghosts from all over the world came and the skill level kept Eric on his toes. Being dead had never been so lively.

Just as he was about to enter the room through the window, he caught the sound of a man singing, "I found love in the back"— Eric stopped mid-flight—"of my blue truck." What the …?

They never had music on when they played cards. Eric diverted his route to the front of the house and peered in through the window. Seeing nobody, he entered and followed the music.

In the kitchen he found a woman. Not just any woman. A *real* woman, full-figured with curves a man could grab hold of. Long, honey colored hair fell in thick waves to her shoulders. Perfection. Fine wisdom lines radiated from her cat-shaped eyes, which were the soft green of sage in the morning sun and her full mouth made him yearn to be alive. He liked his women strong and mature and she was all that and more. He sighed. Too bad her taste in music sucked.

Lilith rubbed against his leg, purring. He reached down and scratched her ears, which made her purr more, so he lifted a finger to his mouth. Not impressed, the cat lifted her tail into the air and strutted off.

Abby's cell phone rang. She turned off the music and answered. "What's wrong?"

"The baby. Her temperature isn't coming down."

Tears welled in the woman's eyes. "I have another hour to work."

"But the baby."

"What's her temperature?"

"It came down a half degree, but that's still pretty high."

"Bathe her with a cold washcloth. If it doesn't help, put her in a cold bath. I'll be home as soon as I can. I need this job to pay for her meds."

No answer.

"Can you do that for me? Please. I beg you. One more hour." Tears trickled down her alabaster-white cheeks. He checked her hands. No rings.

"All right."

"You're the best cousin ever. Love you." She put the phone down.

Eric lifted the boiling kettle and poured the water into Abby's tea pot, which already contained a tea ball. The aroma of high mountain oolong tea lifted into the air.

~

*A*bby wiped at her tears and sniffed. Oolong tea and wood smoke? The aromas became stronger. Was that a man-scent mixed with the wood smoke? She shook her head. Not having slept for a week was rattling her nerves.

Laughter erupted in the third room.

Abby growled. Ignoring the noise, she reached for the kettle. But … it had moved. She could have sworn she put it on the right front burner and now it was on the left. She looked at her tea pot. Steam rose through its snout. That explained the tea smell. Had she already poured it? And forgotten? What the heck?

A cold chill danced at the base of her skull. The room seemed cooler too. Could it be a ghost? She couldn't hold that thought in her head. No way. No how. She didn't have time for a ghost. If there was a ghost, she might scream. But no. There could be no ghost. Being so worn out, she must have forgotten she had poured the water. That's all.

She shrugged. *Reality really doesn't matter. Only my perception of it does.* Or so she mumbled to herself. Her choice was simple: believe a ghost had poured her tea and scream or drink the tea. Gosh darn … Her life had never been easy, so why should it start being so now.

If there were a spirit or two here, so be it. As long as they didn't hurt her, she wouldn't hurt them. The knot in her stomach tightened. Obviously her body didn't get the message.

Focus, Abigail. Focus. She poured a cup of tea and reached into the garbage. After a couple minutes of searching, she pulled out the remnants of a sandwich. Ham and cheese. For the next ten minutes she sipped tea and feasted on her scavenged dinner, determined to make the best of her life.

~

*K*nowing the house well, Eric flew behind her back to the far side of the room, opened up a cupboard and pulled out a package of cookies. He flew back and slid them on top of the counter, beside her.

When Abby reached for her cup, she saw the biscuits. She looked around with wide eyes, and then opened the box and ate three. The moaning sound that came from her lips made him shudder. The rest of the cookies, she poured into her purse. After scanning the room, she picked up her broom and began sweeping the floor, humming that crappy song he had heard earlier.

The woman fascinated him. And it certainly wasn't her singing. He spent the next hour watching her finish her chores and followed her home to make sure she was safe.

And see where she lived.

CHAPTER 3

TO SERVE AND PROTECT

Dressed in his police uniform Zane Carrington slammed his front door behind him. Nothing had been going his way, not this day, this week, this year … effin'-hell … this life. He cursed as he stowed his gun in the lock box in the drawer of his entrance table. Being a cop was a hard job, but being a bad cop was proving to be even harder.

The air of the small bungalow cooled as a current of mist swirled around him. The dust particles within it shimmered like black crystals in sunlight.

"I'm trying," he said. "I'm trying."

The dark air stilled and manifested into a ghostly specter. "Not hard enough." The poltergeist's voice echoed cold and deadly through the main room as if he were the devil himself.

"I have my eye on a family new to town. There are three children under the age of five and the mother is a widow. Her cousin comes and goes, but the woman is alone most of the time and she goes out at night."

"Where does she go?"

"She's the new cleaner at the teahouse."

"Rufus's teahouse? How interesting."

"Does that make a difference?"

"No. Yes. I'm not sure. But …" The air turned cooler as the grumbling sound of the evil spirit rumbled through his wooden, craftsman style home, as if it were an aftershock from a major earthquake. "It would be even sweeter to take a child from under the noses of those self-righteous ghosts."

Zane shrugged. How the hell did he get himself into this? He trembled as sweat poured off his body.

His face must have given away his terror. "Don't go getting second thoughts," said the dark spirit as it moved closer to him and stopped within an inch of his nose. A swirling mini-tornado of damp, dark energy it smelled like putrid flesh. With a black flash, it manifested into a twelve-year old bully of a boy with faded freckles on a round, pudgy face, big ears and a cowlick. Black, beady eyes drenched Zane with a wave of coldness that pulled him, as if it were a rip-tide, into a vat of endless, mirthless evil, a glimpse of hell itself.

Shuddering, Zane swallowed hard, and took a step back, hoping it wouldn't go inside him again. "No. No. We have a deal. I'll do my part."

"Yes, you will." The ghost chuckled. "Or else I will re-enter your daughter Rebecca and this time I won't leave."

CHAPTER 4

I DON'T BELIEVE IN GHOSTS

At three in the morning, Jane's fever broke and Abby did her victory dance, an arms-in- the-air-wiggle everything kind of jig. They had won another battle. That was what her life seemed these days, one battle after another in a long and arduous war for survival. If she were on her own, she would have given up long ago, but she had three kids and she would do whatever it took to give them a good life. Not that she was a perfect mom, or a perfect person for that matter; just that she knew what she had to do.

Starting with food. She put half the cookies from the teahouse on the pillow of five-year old, Jonathan, and the other half on the pillow of his three-year old sister, Jinx. They had a JJ theme going on in the family. She smiled as she looked at them. No matter how crazy wild they could be during the day, at night they looked so angelic when they slept. It brought tears to her eyes. The universe may have dealt her a hard hand, but she had been given the sweetest children in the world and she was truly blessed.

After she tucked them in, she went to the kitchen table

and turned on her lap top. She wanted to work a few hours on her manuscript. Was she being selfish taking this time for herself? Maybe, but she couldn't help it. She loved to write and if she didn't, she felt incomplete. At five in the morning she dragged herself to bed. It felt as if she had just closed her eyes when she awoke to the kids bouncing on her bed. They had found the cookies.

"Mommy, mommy." Jinx nudged her shoulder.

"I'm glad you like them honey, but I need a little bit more—"

Bang! Bang! Bang!

Who would be at her front door this early in the morning?

Abby grabbed her terry-cloth robe as she went to the front door. When she opened it, a cool February breeze off the strait nipped her face. But no one was there. She tasted the salt in the air as she looked around. The other houses on the street looked quiet. The low winter light gave everything around her a warm glow. It had to be near freezing. She looked down at her bare feet, which were particularly cold, and saw a brown-paper, shopping bag sitting on her doorstep.

Of all the crazy things!

After looking around one more time, she bent over and inspected the bag. It was loaded with food: bread, and bottles of jam and peanut butter stuck out the top. She picked it up and went back inside the house. Inside the bag she found: bread, butter, jam, peanut butter, cheese, bananas, strawberries, ground beef and a dozen eggs. Abby swallowed. The kids would eat a real meal today. There was enough food here to last until she got her first paycheck. She wouldn't have to visit the food bank.

A tingling sensation crawled across her scalp. It wasn't the generosity of the gift, or the strange way it had suddenly appeared, that made her feel uneasy. It was the visceral feeling that someone was near, watching them. Was that wood smoke she smelled? Again. She shook her head, hoping it might help her think.

Jonathan with cookie crumbs all over his PJs jumped up and down beside her. "We have breakfast."

Jinx stood on her other side beaming. "I'm hungry Mommy."

So Abby carefully put the food away and put a frying pan on the burner. They would have scrambled eggs, with toast and jam. It had been three days since she'd a full meal; one since the kids had.

~

*E*ric stood in the kitchen, watching in silence. Having died young, he had never had the opportunity to raise a family of his own, and watching these kids go at the food gave him a warm feeling, the kind he imagined fathers felt. The best part was seeing color return to their cheeks. These people had been hungry for awhile.

He followed them to the park later, where the kids played for a couple hours. They returned to have a big lunch. Abby listened to every story they told her, cared for their every need. She was an amazing mother, so full of love.

In the afternoon the kids played in the living room, while the baby slept and Abby typed on a beat-up laptop. The thought that he was basically stalking them flashed through his mind, but he shrugged it off. He wasn't hurting anyone.

Wondering what she was doing on the computer, Eric moved closer to Abby. Her earthy scent held him. Not pretentious, or too sweet, just earthy. Peering over her shoulder he read the words on the screen. The top line read: "Who Killed the Butler?" The words made little sense to him, but how her body, her luscious body, relaxed when she typed, did. She loved writing as much as she loved her kids. Her phone rang.

"Hi Jillian. Good to hear from you," she said. Her cell phone wasn't on speaker, so he couldn't hear the reply, but he was glad it wasn't a man. Glad? Why should he care?

"No … yes … no … maybe … Listen, you wouldn't believe what happened to me today." Abby told the other woman about the groceries.

"What? … Are you kidding? … No, I won't quit my job … Seriously? … I don't care what stories you've heard about the teahouse. I don't believe in ghosts."

CHAPTER 5

JUST ANOTHER NIGHT IN A HAUNTED TEAHOUSE

With the clear sky, the night turned cool and crisp. Abby arrived at the teahouse at ten o'clock. Jillian was taking care of the kids. It wasn't a permanent solution to her child-minding needs, but it worked for now.

Jillian wanted Abby to quit the job, but that wasn't going to happen. She needed it too badly. The stories about the place were undoubtedly exaggerated, and Abby refused to believe them, no matter how many there were.

Ten o'clock seemed like a good time to start. The mysterious activity in the third room happened the last night around midnight. By that time, she would have most of her work done. Not that she believed in ghosts, but she would rather avoid whatever was going on in that room.

The nightly visitors had to be regular, flesh-and-blood people who snuck in to the teahouse party. If she could get most of her work done before they arrived, she would be less inclined to open the forbidden door. It seemed like a practical solution.

Abby heard noise in the back of the house and headed for the kitchen. Wait …What the hell was she thinking? There was no way anyone could have snuck into that room without her seeing them. Unless there was a trap door to the basement, or maybe a root cellar, or they used the window, or … She shook her head. *I don't believe in ghosts. End of story.*

Azalea emerged from the basement with a large cardboard box marked with an enormous red heart on the outside. "Here you are Abby: decorations for Valentine's Day."

Abby took one end of the box, and helped her place it on the counter.

"I was hoping you would have time to start putting them up tonight." She took off the top of the box and they both peered in. I like to hang red hearts with satin ribbon from the ceiling, and place Valentine-themed centerpieces on each of the tables."

"Sure, no problem." Except, of course it was. What single woman with no date, or hope of a date for Valentine's wants to put up hearts? That is unless they're broken. But the paper hearts would help her get a paycheck. She smiled at the decorations.

"Good. I'll let you figure out where to hang them."

"Just not in the third room. Right?"

Azalea gave her the stink eye. She was darn good at it too. "Not the third room."

Abby grinned as if it were a joke between them.

But Azalea did not smile back. "I'm off then."

After her boss left, the teahouse fell silent. Funny how some places can feel quieter than others. This place had its own personality, and maybe it was just her over-active imagination, but it seemed to inhale the quiet, to feed on it, as if it were preparing for something more. Something perhaps on the slippery side of normal. Creepy didn't begin to explain the feeling that nibbled on the edges of her senses.

Get a grip.

The house enveloped her with a stone-cold silence, a graveyard quiet and Abby shivered in its embrace.

She pulled a decoration out of the box. It was a red, paper heart the size of her hand, attached to a long ribbon. It would look pretty hanging from the ceiling. It reminded her of Valentine's Days in her past. A smell caught her attention and she put the heart back into the box.

The same peculiar odor she had noticed the night before hung in the air, but it seemed more distinct this time, stronger, perhaps because she wasn't as nervous, or perhaps because she wasn't twisted with worry, or perhaps because she had a full belly. Who knows why we perceive what we do, when we do?

At least the smell didn't include the foul stench of a cigar. Maybe that came later. She took a long breath in. Mold, mildew . . . mothballs . . . and wood smoke.

As she hung up her jacket an icy breeze drifted across her shoulders. *I don't believe in ghosts,* she told herself as if that would stop the fear building inside her.

She took out her cell phone and hit her radio app, set for 105.3, Rockin' Wild Country. Singing as loudly as she could, she set about her cleaning.

Lilith eyed her suspiciously when she entered her room and then stood up, stretched her back in an arch and went back to sleep.

Nothing else jarred her as she cleaned and polished every surface in sight. A nasty, sticky stain on the floor kept her attention for ten minutes. She had to use straight dish detergent to loosen its grip. Maybe it was orange juice. Her nerves remained on edge, but she could live with that. Just before midnight she decided to take her break.

As she passed the third door she heard a man call out, "Cheater. There can't be five aces in a deck." A chorus of laughter broke out. More yelling. A card game? Her unwanted guests had arrived.

"Go ahead and take my chips if you want." Silence fell. "I'll have your head."

A tingling sensation, as if a dozen spiders raced across her scalp, made her throat go dry. Her stomach dropped. It couldn't be ghosts. Even if they did exist, they wouldn't play cards. Would they? And ghosts wouldn't joke about taking heads, because they had none, or at least she didn't think they did. If ghosts existed, they would be out haunting something.

Not her.

She shook her head. Okay, so they're not ghosts. Then they must be human, live ones, that is. Whether Azalea knew it or not, a secret poker game was being played in her house. That was the answer. She stood outside the door wanting to open it, wanting to make sure that indeed the gamblers were made of flesh and blood. But she had made a promise and she always kept her promises. Gritting her teeth, she walked past the door.

When she got to the kitchen, the kettle was at full boil. "Oh sweet baby Jesus!" If she'd had something in her hands, she would have dropped it. Her head swiveled from side to side. But no one was there. At least no one she could see.

Hail Mary, Jesus, Buddha and Hari Krishna. Help me, for I am a dimwitted sinner . . .

More laughter from the room shattered her thoughts. She swallowed down her fear, because she had to. Pouring the hot water into the small pot that already had a full tea ball sitting in it, she drew in a slow breath and counted to ten. She would do this. One … two … three …

The scent of a man and wood smoke hit her senses.

Oh for all that is holy, this can't be happening. She needed to be rational, logical like Spock. Cool heads prevail, or so they say. If there were ghosts in the third room, so be it. They weren't hurting her. If they were human, ditto. All she needed to do was keep her head down and get her work done. Spit and polish, that was what she needed to do. Spit and polish. That was her ticket to survival.

But who the hell put the kettle on?

The first sip of tea steadied her nerves. The blend had a punch that lifted her spirits, or maybe it was the caffeine. She could mainline caffeine right now.

Thinking about the baby and her kids calmed her. It had been a good night. Being able to feed them made her feel as though she had turned life around, as though she could be the mother she wanted to be, or at least a shadow of her. She wished she could thank the person who had so generously left them food. Someday she would pay that favor forward.

~

*E*ric watched the smile grow on Abby's lips as she swallowed her tea. He wondered how they would taste. Sweet like honey, he imagined. The laughter in the poker room called to him and he decided to play a few hands, but before he left he swung closely by Abby to take in her earthy scent. What a woman.

~

*C*old air ruffled through Abby's hair, as if she stood in the wind, but the air in the room was still. Abby swallowed. This had to be the most unusual job she had ever had, or ever heard of for that matter. After rubbing the goosebumps on her arms, she set about finding food.

Half a sandwich lay near the top of the garbage and it smelled okay. She bit into it. Mmm. Cucumber and cream cheese had never tasted so good. All she had left to do were the washrooms, and then she would call it a night and get home to her family.

If she could just get the noise from the third room out of her mind, everything would be perfect. She turned up the music on her cell phone.

As she scrubbed the first toilet, she heard a blood-curdling cry of pain.

It sounded as if a woman had been stabbed. It came from *that* room.

Azalea told me not to go in there, no matter what I hear. But someone's hurt. She couldn't expect me to let that happen. I can't stand by ...

"Ahh! Stop that," screamed a woman.

With a string mop in her hand, Abby ran to the third door. The screaming stopped. Pressing her ear to the old-wood surface she could hear voices, the sound of cards being shuffled and poker chips being thrown in a pile. More laughter. Sinister laughter. Jovial laughter. And chatter.

Then Bang! A gun shot.

Her hand trembled next to the door handle. How could she ignore a gun shot? But she had to.

Abby stood listening for fifteen minutes, the longest fifteen minutes in her life. No more screams. No more threats. No more gun shots. Just the sound of people playing cards, people who weren't supposed to be there. She strained to hear more. If someone was hurt, they wouldn't continue their game, would they?

Unless they were already dead.

Spock would deduce at this point that the presence of

ghosts was indeed a logical conclusion, but she just couldn't go there. Ghosts belonged to Halloween, not to her world.

"The cleaning lady's listening," said one of the gamblers. Abby took a step back and looked at the door. They knew she was there. They knew she was listening.

Who the hell were they?

CHAPTER 6

THIRD ROOM TO THE RIGHT

On the third night, Abby sang as she walked up the long front stairs to the teahouse. Life was good. The kids had eaten three meals and snacks for two days, she had a job and her butler mystery had finally taken shape. The teahouse ghosts or whatever they were had not bothered her, or at least not yet.

Before using her keys, she stopped to listen to the house. The more she thought about it, the more she figured the place had a personality of its own. It liked being clean and organized. She swore it had its own way of sighing when she finished her work, as if its pride hung in the lightness of the air, and the house shifted on its foundations to soak in more moonlight. She shook her head. People would think her crazy if they knew she thought the house had feelings, but this one did.

And then there were the gamblers . . .

So she stood in the front foyer taking in the mood of the teahouse. In the pressing darkness, it felt like a sanctuary from the cold of the winter weather outside. As strange as it could be around midnight, it felt welcoming now.

Flicking on the lights, she assessed the work ahead of her. The place was as a quiet and still as a catacomb. Dust in the air shifted under the lighting, glimmering as if it were magic. A heavy sense of foreboding puddled in her stomach. She hugged herself and exhaled. In three hours, she would be free again and one day closer to a paycheck.

$\sim$

The sound of the kettle boiling brought her to the kitchen two hours later. A full tea ball had been set in the small pot that sat beside a pretty tea cup. The charm of the old china pattern warmed her to the thought of a good cuppa. The room smelled of a wood fire, but she knew there was none. She shrugged.

The old, stainless-steel kettle whistled. If it were plugged into the wall like a drip coffee maker with a timer, she could understand how it knew when she needed a break, but it wasn't. It definitely wasn't. A breeze tousled her hair and she swiped at her forehead. "Thanks for the tea," she said out loud. Someone must be in the house. Maybe one of the gamblers. That had to be it.

The pot rose into the air and moved towards her tea pot. She swallowed. As the hot water flowed into the pot the bouquet of high-mountain oolong tea filled the air. What a treat. Whoever her companion was, he knew his tea. She tried to smile at her own joke, but goosebumps pebbled along her arms and the fine hair on the nape of her neck stood up.

How could a kettle of boiling water fly through the air?

The stories about this place varied, but the common theme was that ever since Azalea's brother Rufus died here, ghosts had made it a favorite hangout. And those ghosts could get rowdy. For the most part the rumors weren't all that terrifying. She poured milk into her tea. That is, if you could say a story about dead people moving around wasn't scary. She stirred. There had been many drive by sightings of glowing eyes. People had heard the laughter and the screams. But no one had been hurt.

"I said, thank you," she said.

A bag of sugar lifted into the air and tilted releasing a cup of sugar onto the counter.

Abby took a step back. *What the heck!*

The sugar shifted, as if an invisible hand was drawing in it. She looked closer and made out the words, "You're welcome."

"I don't believe in ghosts," she said aloud.

The sugar moved some more. "Boo."

Her heart jack-hammered against her chest. Whether she wanted to believe it or not, someone, or something, made the sugar move.

"Aaah," that blood-curdling scream came again from the third room.

With her mop in her hand, she ran to its door and touched the doorknob. It felt colder than ice, but she turned it anyway. Enough of this nonsense. She needed to get to the bottom of whatever was going on in this house. And darn it to hell, she still refused to believe it was ghosts. As the gut-wrenching screams continued, she turned the knob all the way.

CHAPTER 7

BEHIND DOOR NUMBER THREE

As Abby opened the door a blast of ice-cold air slapped her face. Her breath caught in her throat. Her thoughts flew in all directions. But the room was empty.

Except for the laughter.

It sounded as though a table full of people sat in front of her, and they were all laughing. Then came the sound of small objects hitting the table, as if ghostly poker chips were falling.

"Enough," she said as she increased the grip on her mop. "I don't want anyone hurt on my shift."

More laughter.

Clearly, that didn't work. *Oh my gosh.* They were even more deaf than children. "Are you listening to me?"

Silence.

She put her free hand on her hip. "Is anyone hurt?" She had to ask, even though she hated the way her voice sounded small and goosebumps pebbled the skin on her arms. No doubt her face had gone beet-red too. She gasped for air.

"Enough. Enough already, you ghostly beasts. I heard a woman scream and it sounded like she was in pain."

Silence.

"Excruciating pain."

Silence.

"And who the hell is making me tea?" Her words came out as scrambled as her thoughts and she bit her lip to stop from saying anything more.

A man shimmered into view beside her.

"Oh ... holy hell!" Abby's mouth dropped open. He was a ... No, he couldn't be. But he was. Oh, sweet baby Jesus. He was a Viking.

Built like a Norse god, his seven feet of muscle towered above her. His shoulder length blond hair looked real enough to touch and his roguish, blue eyes held a decidedly-naughty glint. His chest was bare and he wore a fur cloak and leather skirt. "I put the kettle on." The sound of his voice spiked her pulse—low, male and oh so sexy.

"Thanks," she said.

"They call me Dodger."

"Dod ... ger?" That didn't sound like a Viking name.

A woman's voice came out of the cold nothingness around them. "That's what we call him, cuz he's been dodging the light for so long, dearie." She gave a bawdy laugh fitting for a drunken, lady of the night. "And he's good at dodging it."

"Dodging the light? As in The Light?"

The Viking nodded, as his gorgeous eyes caressed her body, not in a lewd way, though she wasn't sure a ghost could be considered lewd, but in a saucy way, the kind that feeds a woman's heart and ignites her passion. Her blood warmed. *Shut the door!* Who knew a ghost could have enough raw sex appeal to weaken a woman knees? Abby exhaled slowly and lifted her chin, determined to enunciate a full sentence. "What the hell are you doing in *my* teahouse?"

The ghosts she couldn't see laughed, and the side of Dodger's mouth quirked up.

She raised a brow.

"Forgive us for laughing." He lifted his hand in a stop gesture. "You have to understand, we think it's funny that you call this teahouse yours. We think of it as ours. Most of us have been coming here for five years, ever since our friend Rufus died in this room. That's what all the screaming is about, by the way."

"The blood-curdling scream?"

"Yeah, that one. It's part of a reenactment of the night Rufus was shot and it happens every night at thirteen past midnight.

She dropped her arms. "Rufus, I'm sorry." Having to die all over again every night had to bite.

Dodger's eyes softened. "Well, he was cheating, so while his death came sooner than he would have liked, it was predictable."

"No sympathy for cheaters."

Dodger looked over at the empty space. "Something like that."

"Is he here now?"

The Viking nodded. "He haunts this house day and night, and holds card games most evenings. We've had a lot of fun here ..."

Grumbling from the invisible crowd of ghosts stopped him.

"Well, except for the one night when two poltergeists muscled in, but that's another story."

"And Azalea doesn't mind?"

"Rufus is Azalea's brother, and being a medium she can see us all. She lets us be. So you see, we think of the teahouse as our place. Usually we play cards late at night, so we don't bother anyone." He hesitated a heartbeat. "But truly, the house and the magical land beneath it belongs to no one."

Abby tilted her head. "I swear it has a mind of its own."

Dodger lifted his perfectly chiseled chin. "You are not only beautiful, but you are also wise. The house is shall we say—charmed." The corners of his eyes crinkled as he smiled. Despite his enormous size, and his silvery glow, he seemed a perfect gentleman. Not scary at all. She inhaled his manly scent and reminded herself that he … was … dead. So why were butterflies dancing in her belly?

"Uh, thank you," she said. *I think. What does one say when a hot ghost feeds you a line?* "Are you flirting with me?" She loosened her hold on the mop handle.

As Dodger moved closer he lowered his smoother than velvet voice, "Let me walk you home tonight." His raw alpha-maleness tingled her senses. Did ghosts have the power to glamor? Or was it his rugged good looks that made her female parts sing? Alive or dead—what did it matter?—this guy had seriously sexy mojo.

Uh-huh, she could guess how he dodged the light, and even though he intrigued her—to put her physical response to him mildly—he wasn't the sort of man—um, ghost —she wanted around her kids. "Nah-uh. That wouldn't be appropriate."

"Appropriate?" As he squinted his brows scrunched to form a V. The scruff on his face looked so real, she wanted to touch it. Feel it against her own face.

Hmm. Turning him down would be stupid. A handsome, scratch that—drop-dead, drool-worthy, wickedly-hot—man wanted to take a walk with her. What could go wrong? "Okay. If you promise to behave."

Dodger gave her a bad-boy smile. "Only if I have to."

CHAPTER 8

DEATH'S A BITCH

The instant Abby left the room the house lights flickered. She needed to write this phenomenon down. The house had its own way of responding to the life and death within it. If she deciphered its responses, she would have a better understanding of what was going on around her. But what the heck did that matter? *Get a grip, woman. Your job is to spit and polish.*

Sucked out of the room by the Valkyrie, Brunhilde, Dodger found himself spit onto the cold, damp, stone floor of her cave dwelling. Being a ghost he didn't feel the fall in his muscles or on his skin, but it dented his ego none the less. *Brunhilde, the bitch of death!*

Not only was Brunhilde his personal shrink, she was also his former mother in-law.

Her burning red eyes glared at him. "What in Odin's name do you think you're doing?" She floated above him.

Her other-worldly voice made him cringe and he shook

his head trying to rid himself of it. In all the centuries he had roamed the earth, he had never heard anyone else screech in such a high-pitched, glass-breaking voice. It echoed through his consciousness grating on the edges of his soul.

Her ancient hand reached out of her black cloak. With a craggy finger she pointed at him. "You need to listen."

"Playing poker. You know I do that. It passes the time." He rose and stared down at her, but she lifted her arm, and with a flash of her magic placed him beneath her, as if he were a bothersome housefly she could bat around.

Brunhilde stood ten-feet tall, but it wasn't her size that gave her power. She had serious, supernatural moxie, a breath that smelled like a sewage pit and a wicked disposition. Her red eyes shone with an unearthly glow as if they were lighthouse beacons for wayward souls. Her scraggly, dirty-blond hair framed a long, pale face dominated by a bulbous nose. Wiry, black hairs sprouted out of her nostrils.

Odin had commanded Brunhilde to fix Dodger centuries ago and her failure to do so, bothered her. Deeply. On more than one occasion, Eric had told her he didn't like being a crochet project for a soul-eating witch, but sensing the chill in the air, he figured such humor would not be wise tonight.

The Valkyrie shimmered blue. "You belong with your own kind."

The Viking rose slowly, expecting to be slammed down at any second. "I spend most of my time with other ghosts."

Like a flame fed pure oxygen, the red in her eyes glowed extra strong. "The woman is human."

So wonderfully human. "She's a widow with three children. I want to make things easier for her. Surely there's no crime in that."

"Why? Why do you want to help *this* one?"

Thoughts flew through his mind: *Because something about her pulls me like a magnet. Her strength. Her courage. Her sense of humor. Her determination. Her beauty. I'm not really sure, but I want to get to know her.* But he said none of that. "Life is hard. If I can make it easier for one person, then I think it's a good day."

The menace in her eyes diminished. "That sounds . . . " She hesitated and looked beyond him as if she were communicating directly with Odin over an invisible hot-line. "Like you're growing up."

Eric laughed. "It happens to the best of us."

"Well, handsome, while I admire your gallant gesture towards the widow— "

"Abigail," he interrupted.

"Abigail, yes. While I admire your desire to help Abigail and her wee ones, I have concerns."

"Now you're beginning to sound like my mother-in-law again. Puritanical, obstinate and crazy. I won't—I can't, as you well know—touch her."

"Perhaps. But if there was a way, I'm sure you would find it."

A ghostly light bulb flashed in his mind. So there was a way? After all the years they had known each other, he could read her well, but he said nothing choosing to file that piece of information, as incredible as it was, away for later.

"I'm not a prude, Eric. And my daughter, your wife, found peace without you centuries ago. Those are not my issues."

"Then what's your problem?"

"I'm not comfortable with ghost-human relationships. They rock the balance of the universe and blur the edges of our five dimensions. They just aren't right."

He knew better than to comment on her prejudice. "I want to help her."

"Hmm. Help someone in need? You may be more ready for the light than you or I ever expected."

"So let me be."

Brunhilde scowled and folded her arms across her chest. "I'm not happy about this."

"I get that."

"I'll make you a deal."

Deal? This should be interesting. He waited while she floated around him twice and stopped a couple inches from his face.

"I won't bother you about this … this … improper dalliance between you and a human woman, if you promise me to finish it within a week."

He nodded, but he seriously doubted that was going to happen.

CHAPTER 9

GETTING TO KNOW YOU

A Viking … and a hot one. Just her luck he was dead.

Abby's mind reeled as she finished her last chores for the night and the time for her walk with Dodger neared. Digging deep to find some humor to lighten the tingle of terror that skittered around her senses, she came up with a new mantra: *I can live with ghosts.* Not that she was sure she could, but it seemed as if the universe had decided she must. *Fate is a bitch.*

When she came out of the bathroom with her mop and pail, she ran right into him. As her body touched his apparition, a chill gripped the base of her spine and spiraled upwards. She stepped back. "Sorry," she said.

"You ready yet?" he said, looking closely at her mop. "I hope you don't plan on using that on me."

"Hi," she said and swallowed.

"You do remember our date."

Date? He's calling this a date. She pulled her hand through her hair, hoping it didn't look as messy as she imagined it must. "Give me five."

"I'll wait for you outside the front door," he said and

walked past her. *Hmm, nice back side. Hard and round. Oh my goodness what am I thinking?* She shook her head and headed to the janitor's closet to put things away. Cold, as in dead cold. That was how he felt. Dead. She needed to remember that.

A few minutes later she joined Eric on the front porch. As she stepped down the stairs he kept pace with her, floating by her side.

It was a gorgeous night, warm for February, with a clear sky filled with stars and a full moon. It was a lover's sky. *He's dead*, she reminded herself.

"So they call you Dodger," she said out loud.

"*Ja*, my friends call me that, but my real name is Erik Eklund. I am from Sweden and I am a Viking warrior."

"And you dodge the light."

He looked up at the stars and her eyes followed. He sighed. "Something like that. But tell me more about you."

"My name is Abigail Jenkins. Friends call me Abby. I hope you'll call me Abby." The words flowed out of her mouth as if she were talking … as if she were talking to a real guy. She tossed her hair behind her shoulders. "I feel so silly."

"Don't," he said. "It's just you and me. Let's just be our selves, our true selves."

The timbre of his voice resonated within her, masculine … strong … and oh so sexy. This had to be the craziest experience she had ever had, but the sincerity in his voice anchored her. There was no point in lying to a dead man. "I'm a widow and I have three children under the age of five. You can run now. Or float away, or whatever ghosts do when they want to escape a complicated situation."

"*I*'m not going anywhere."

The megawatt smile he gave her warmed her from the ring on her baby toe to the top of her head. Not exactly the response one usually had when a ghost tells you he's sticking around. But this guy, this ghost, this whatever, was something else. "Uh-huh," was all she could manage to say.

~

*E*ric wanted to tell her that he thought he was the strongest and bravest women he had ever met, but he didn't want her to know he had already been in her home and seen her family and the hard road they traveled. She would feel stalked. And while stalking was quite acceptable in his world, it wasn't in hers. He needed to be careful what he said, so he said nothing.

Part of him, the practical part that he rarely listened to, thought this walk would cool his interest in her. After all, he had met many beautiful women over the years who seemed much less beautiful when they started talking. But this one was different. Everything about her was different. She had a brave and warm heart.

After a hot, uncomfortable minute, he broke their silence. "What happened to your husband?"

"Ben." She bit her lip. After a second's hesitation, she continued, "had brain cancer." She swallowed. The memories of his illness and his death, still so fresh and painful made her stop in her tracks for a minute. Eric stood beside her and said nothing.

"Between you and me," she continued as she started walking again, "he could have lived longer. He gave up on life."

"I can't imagine him wanting to leave you."

"It wasn't me. It was the drugs and the never-ending tests. Cancer is a horrible way to die. It takes you down bit by bit. He got tired of fighting and just wanted it all to stop." She shrugged as if the action could rid her of her feelings. "I know I'm supposed to feel sorry for him, but I don't. I'm angry as hell at him. He gave up."

"Did he have a choice?"

She nodded. Her throat thickened. "There was one more experimental drug he could have tried. I don't understand why he wouldn't give it a chance. He left me to raise the kids alone. He could have given our family one more try."

Eric said nothing, just stayed beside her as she spilled her guts all over the city sidewalk. After a few seconds he flew behind her and came up on her other side. "You shouldn't beat yourself up for feelings that are so natural. Death is hard on all of us."

"You must think I'm a horrid person. Normally I hide behind a mask, but you're not human, or at least not … Well you know what I mean. I'm sure you couldn't care less about the details of my predicament."

Eric winced. *And you would be wrong.* But he nodded hoping she would reveal more of herself. When she didn't, he spoke. "I don't understand how a man would leave you, not to mention his three children, if he felt he had a choice. I suspect Ben had come to the end of his road. He made the best choice he could."

She kicked a stone with her toe. "Ben stayed alive until I had the baby and then he stopped eating, and a few days later they pronounced him dead." He had chosen his time yes, but it would be a long time before she would forgive him for it.

"Abby, it's not your fault. None of it's your fault. Not his cancer. Not his death. And not your anger. Give yourself a break."

She stopped and looked into the Viking's blue eyes, the color of the sky on a clear spring morning. A woman could get lost in those peepers if she weren't careful. What was it she was trying to say? Darn those eyes. They made her feel as though tropical ocean waves washed over her, warming her, caressing her, washing away her pain. If she weren't careful his baby blues would carry her off to sea.

She swallowed. Yup, she had spilled her guts. And nope, he hadn't run. "Thanks for listening."

He shrugged.

"Do you think Ben is around?" Abby looked into the dark night.

"We're alone right now." Eric kept pace with her. "That's all I can really say. Who lives and who dies and where they roam is beyond my understanding."

"But you would feel him, if he were near."

"Ja."

"Ah well. He probably took the express bus upstairs, being raised a good Catholic boy and all."

Dodger nodded. "Most people take the express, one way or another."

"But not you."

His jaw clenched. "Back to you. Raising three kids is hard. Do you have any family that can help you?

"My cousin, Jillian. She's all I got, but she's darn special." Abby waved her hand in the air. "She and her husband Mike moved here last fall, so after Ben died I came to town to be near them. Jillian babysits for me and helps me out as much as she can. But that's enough about me. Your turn. How old are you?"

"The dead don't tell time." He tilted his head, a smile tugging on his perfect lips. "It passes differently in our dimension. But I can tell you I was born in the tenth century, before the Norman conquest of England."

"You're over a thousand years old!"

"Ja, and I'm a 1B ghost, which means I'm powerful."

And humble too, she thought.

"The one means I can manifest in human form at any time, to anyone I choose. The B part means I'm benevolent. I would never hurt you or anyone else."

"So if you're so powerful, why don't you go to heaven?"

He paused a moment and then spoke in a quieter voice, as if he had decided to tell her something he didn't like to talk about. "As a young man I dreamed of going to Valhalla. That is where Vikings who die in battle go. But that was not my good fortune. So I continue here on earth where I have fun."

"So you didn't die in battle."

"Nej." A dark shadow crossed his eyes warning her not to ask more.

A little breeze ruffled Abby's hair and she eyed him.

"You know in all my years I have never met a woman like you."

Abby put her hand up for him to stop. "Don't."

"Why not? I thought we would speak true."

And sometimes a man and a woman need a little mystery. But she didn't say that. She stopped in front of her little house. She knewit looked like a rundown shack to most people, but to her it was home. "Here we are. I would invite you in, but …"

Her words were interrupted by a loud, female scream coming from inside her house.

CHAPTER 10

AN UNWANTED GHOST

As Abby fumbled with keys, Eric walked through the door into the front room.

He couldn't believe his eyes. Pure, black energy swirled around a woman. A poltergeist! The woman had stopped screaming and looked unconscious. With her eyes wide-open she had slid into the poltergeist's power.

"Poltergeist, be gone," Eric shouted.

The front door opened and Abby ran into the room.

Hearing Eric, the poltergeist's energy stopped swirling and sucked itself back into a human form, a boy with half his head missing. A truly gruesome sight. As he tightened the grip on the woman's neck her face paled to deathly white.

"How dare you interrupt me, Viking."

"You don't belong here." He swiped the air with his massive arm. I vanquish you."

"You cannot." The boy laughed. "You may be bigger than me, but we both know you're not stronger."

"Let the woman go."

Electric energy buzzed through the room

Abby edged to Eric's side. "Sweet Jesus, what the hell is

that." She pointed at the boy, whose ghastly image fazed in and out, looking human one moment and like black mist the next.

"A poltergeist. Let me handle it."

"Making friends with humans, Viking? How cute." The leer on the boy's face chilled the room.

"Be gone. *Dra åt helvete.*"

The boy laughed.

"I said, go to hell."

Abby picked up a lamp from the side table and threatened the poltergeist with it. She didn't really think a lamp could hurt a spirit, but she wasn't about to stand by and watch her cousin die. "In the name of all that is holy, be gone. Get out of my house," she screamed.

The evil spirit evaporated. She rushed in and gathered her cousin in her arms.

"Jillian, are you all right?" Holding her close she felt warmth return to her cousin's cold, body. Jillian coughed. Abby stroked her hair.

Meanwhile the Viking stood beside them and said nothing.

"What? What just happened?" Jillian sputtered as she regained consciousness.

Abby looked up at Eric. He shook his head.

"I'm not sure," said Abby and that was the honest to goodness truth. "When I came in you were ... not looking good. You look better now. Do you remember what happened?"

Jillian pushed herself away and put her hand to her forehead. "The last thing I remember was hearing a noise outside the door. I went to check it out, but before I reached the door ... No, that makes no sense."

"Just tell me what you remember."

"I must have fallen asleep. It must have been a dream. A nightmare."

"Tell me."

"A little black cloud …" She closed her eyes and scrunched up her face. "Came at me and kind of … devoured me. It made horrific slurping sounds as it ate me from the inside out. I screamed and then everything went black." Her body trembled and her face remained an unearthly white color, making her look more dead than Eric. "It had to be a nightmare. The worst ever."

Abby looked again at Eric. He folded his arms in front of his chest and shook his head. Well, maybe he wasn't a hot shot at helping with the living, but it sure had been nice to have him around when she had to deal with that other thing.

Mike, Jillian's husband, came in through the open front door. "What's going on? Why is the door wide open?" Seeing Jillian on the floor, he rushed towards her.

"She's okay. She's going to be okay," Abby said, wanting to believe it, more than actually believing it, herself.

Jillian gave him one of her determined looks "Take me home."

Mike looked over her head at Abby and raised a brow. She gave him a thumbs up.

"Abby, I don't want to leave without knowing what happened. Are the kids okay?" Mike was the uber-responsible one in the family and she loved that about him.

The kids! "I'll check," she said. Eric flew ahead of her down the hall. They checked the bedrooms. All three slept soundly, as if they had no cares in the world.

When she got back to the living room, Jillian was standing on her own. Wobbly, but vertical. That had to be a good sign. Right? Her cheeks had some color, but her eyes still had a nasty yellow glow to them. A hangover from the dark spirit.

"The kids are fine. I can't thank you enough, Jillian, for taking care of them."

She nodded slowly. "Glad to help out."

"Let's go home," said Mike, putting an arm around her waist. Normally Jillian wouldn't have liked that sign of love in public, but she didn't object. Abby saw them to the door and watched them get into their car parked at the curb.

After they re-entered the house, Eric spoke first. "You were amazing."

Abby felt a lot of things, but amazing wasn't one of them. "What was that? Why was it in my home? What the hell just happened?" Anger rose inside her as words gushed out.

"*Älsking,* calm down. You and your children are safe. I am here."

"Great, a ghost guard." Her emotions rampaged within her, tearing her apart, not letting her hide behind a façade of politeness. Was this the cost of taking the janitor job? She wanted to kick him or bite him, or someone, hard. Her home and her family had been assaulted. And Jillian, her sweet cousin who would do anything for her, had been hurt.

"Sit down. I'll make you a cup of tea."

"I don't want tea." She threw her arms in the air. "I want an explanation. What happened?"

"The swirling dark energy was a poltergeist. By his color and abilities, I'd say he's powerful. Very powerful. And mean. And vicious."

"What would he want from me?"

Their eyes locked for a moment. Eric's glacial blues didn't flinch. She could hear the wheels turning in his ghostly noggin, wondering how much to tell her.

"Just tell me."

"He wants your children."

CHAPTER 11

JUST A REGULAR GHOST

"My children? That ... that thing wants my children? What would he do with them?" Air rushed out of her lungs.

"I wish you'd let me make you tea."

"Does he eat kids?"

"How about honey? Would you like honey in your tea?"

She glared at him. "Tell me, or I swear I'll ... I'll ... "

A slow, sly grin spread across his face. "And I thought you couldn't look more beautiful. Did you know that when you get riled up, you're really something? A momma bear. No, more like a panther mom ready to go for the jugular."

"Eric."

He blew wind in her direction, forcing her body backwards, towards the sofa. She sat and folded her arms across her chest. "That's better," he said.

Her hands clenched into fists.

"Have you ever met a poltergeist before?" he asked.

She shook her head.

"Well, for starters, don't believe all the stories you've heard, or the horror movies you've seen. Poltergeists don't come in a one-size package of misery. They come in all sizes and shapes. The most important thing to remember about them is that they are evil, pure evil."

"Are they ghosts?"

His head toggled from side to side. "Nej. I wouldn't call them ghosts. Mostly they're left over anger."

"Anger?"

"Ja, when a person dies with a lot of anger, it can be left behind."

"And they're dangerous."

"I wish you would let me make you a cup of tea."

She shook her head. "Tell me everything you know about poltergeists."

Eric sat beside her on the couch. "They are distinctly different from all other spirit forms, a wicked mixture of negative energies, remnants of anger and hate, too volatile to pass over to higher dimensions. Black to their core."

"And they use this dark energy in our world? My world?"

"It can't leave the mortal plane. It's trapped. Their pain wants to cause more pain. It feeds on pain. Like I said, it's pure evil."

She ran a hand through her hair. How could this be happening? An evil spirit in her house! "So what does he want with my children?"

Eric looked away for a moment as if he considered not answering her question. "Many spirits stay near their death spots or haunt specific locations for reasons of their own. Others, like me, roam. I suspect he roams in search of power."

"Power? Why does he need power?"

"His dark energy needs fuel. I've heard of one who uses ancient, demon magic to satiate his appetite."

"Demon? You're telling me he's part demon."

"Ja, possibly. Demons have many ways to suck on the

essence of humanity, and working through poltergeists is one of them. There is an old story about a poltergeist called Louis Lament who visits this town every five years. He is a local legend. I suspect your poltergeist is him."

"Louis Lament?"

"If rumors are to be believed, he uses demonic powers to feeds on children. They are the purest form of energy. Once fed, he moves on, only to return when his energy lags."

"And no one stops him?"

"You saw him. He's difficult to stop and impossible to capture. Like I said, once he's fed, he disappears. He comes and goes quickly and no one knows where he goes, which makes it difficult to stop him."

"He's hurting innocent children. Doesn't that offend you and your friends? Do you have no humanity left? No moral code?"

"Yes we care, but one thing you learn when you live as long as we have is that you can't fix all the wrongs in the world."

"This is a pretty big one."

Eric looked towards the door. "I will stay and watch over your family tonight. That I can do."

"And tomorrow?"

"If you were any other woman, I would tell you to pack up and leave."

"But you won't."

"I don't want you to leave."

Despite the anger and fear burning inside her, Abby felt a smile on her lips. "Can we get rid of Louis permanently?"

"Telling him to leave worked tonight. You are a brave and bold woman. But, I'm not sure it will work a second time, as he will be prepared for it."

"We have to find a way to stop him. Permanently."

"I wish you would let me make you tea."

Abby got up. "All right, I'll drink tea, but I'm coming with you to help make it." They walked into the kitchen. The irony that she was entertaining a ghost in the middle of the night was not lost on her. "I don't suppose you drink tea?"

"Nej, but I will enjoy watching you drink it." He made a motion with his hands and the kettle filled with water. "Azalea being a medium, might know more about Louis than I do."

"I'll ask her tomorrow. And I'll do a search on the Internet for information on Louis Lament. Will you ask the other ghosts what they know?"

He nodded. "Don't get your hopes up there. No one wants to deal with a poltergeist. They can do unspeakable things to benevolent ghosts like us."

Abby watched him make her tea. A Norse god in her kitchen!

Eric placed the tea pot on the kitchen table and brought her a cup and saucer. "I think a stiff drink might do you more good."

Abby nodded. "There are many children in town. Why did he come to my home?"

He tilted his head as he poured her tea.

Silence filled the room.

"Eric?"

"Are you sure you want to hear this?"

"Hell, yeah. I don't care how bad the news is, I want it straight up. I have to know what I'm dealing with."

"Louis works through other people. I suspect he has someone looking for vulnerable children."

Abby gasped. The puzzle pieces slid into place. Her kids were vulnerable, because they only had her. Fudge. It wasn't fair. She swallowed, but the pain of the realization wouldn't stay down. "Got it."

His scent—all manly-man, mixed with wood fire—

became stronger. "I know you're doing the best you can, but sometimes we all need help."

"What do you suggest?" Lifting the tea cup to her mouth, she noticed her hand trembling.

"Let me help."

What would she tell the kids? Hey, kiddos, we have new babysitter and by the way he's a ghost. This was all too bizarre. After a second she answered him. "I can't see how that could work. You're a ghost."

"True, but I am your ghost and I will do everything I can to protect you and your family." The warmth of his smile heated the entire room.

"You'll watch over us."

He nodded. "Louis won't come back tonight, and if he does, I'll deal with him. Tomorrow you can manage on your own during the day, but you should bring the kids to work with you in the evening."

Would she lose her job if she took her kids to work? Even if Azalea agreed to it, would she get anything done? Cleaning a haunted house was difficult enough with its dirty, creaky floors and blood-curdling screams, without adding little kids and … the undeniable chemistry between her and Eric. Her life was getting more than complicated.

One thing she knew for sure: the poltergeist had to be stopped.

CHAPTER 12

ZANE'S NIGHTMARE

Zane tapped a pen on the desk at the Sunset Cove police station. What the hell could he do? He hadspent his whole career protecting people, and now he was delivering three innocent children to a demonic poltergeist. Great Mountie he turned out to be. Wishing his pen were a bat and the desk the heart of the unholy beast, he tapped harder.

His boss, Molly Enright, strode into his office. "Got nothing better to do than tap your pen?"

He looked her in the eye. If she knew what an asshole he was, she would shoot him on the spot. For that matter, the whole office would. The whole community. No one would ever forgive him for this. Hell, he would never forgive himself for this. Ever.

But he had to protect Rebecca.

"Just collecting my thoughts," he said.

"I didn't know you had any."

The lighthearted jab was all part of the regular office banter, but for the life of him he couldn't think of a suitable barb to volley back at her, so he put his hands up. "You got me."

Molly crossed over to his desk and leaned towards him. In her mid-forties, she was a well-respected, seasoned officer. Her long, black hair was pulled back in a conservative bun, revealing high cheekbones and a thin mouth. She gave him her narrowed-eye cop stare, which had been known to break the hardest of criminals. It cut him like a laser in the dark. "You okay?"

"Hell no. I'm a police officer." That was the best he had. Pitiful, really.

"Uh-huh." Her eyes roved over his face as if his secret could be mined in his features. Suspicion was her middle name, and she was a damn fine detective as a result. "You haven't been yourself for a week. If the circles under your eyes get any bigger you'll lose your nose." She leaned back and snickered. "Though, that might be an improvement."

Zane shrugged. She could say whatever she wanted. Nothing could hurt him now. Nothing could be worse than what was happening to his family.

"Zane, seriously, home trouble? I heard Suzie went to stay with her mother."

His jaw tightened. How she knew his wife had left was a puzzle. But Molly was one hell of a detective. He stopped himself from shrugging again. He needed to de-escalate the situation, throw her curiosity in another direction. Molly would never give up on a mystery until she solved it. "Yeah," he said after a moment. "Family shit. Private, family shit."

Her shoulders relaxed. "Well, if you ever want to talk about it."

He laughed in a teasing way. "Are you thinking of starting a new career as a shrink?"

"Just trying to be a friend." Her eyes narrowed again.

Her cell phone rang and she nodded his way. After

finishing a text message, she turned her attention back to him. "Gotta go. But this—" She pointed at him and then herself— "isn't over. I know something's going down. I can smell it."

Demons do smell like shit. Zane gave her as warm a smile as he could manage. Friends. When she had left his office, he checked his own cell phone. No news. No damn news! If things had gone according to plan, the poltergeist should be feasting on the children by now and his daughter should be free. But she wasn't. Had he devoured all of them? Stone-cold sweat trickled down the back of his neck.

Who makes a pact with a demon and expects him to hold up his end of the bargain? *You're an idiot Zane ... a stupid effin' idiot. With no integrity. No honor. The worst of cowards.*

And his soul?

He hung his head back and he stared at the ceiling. He had gone over this a million times. He had had no choice. Louis made that clear.

No one could help him. Louis had his daughter. He swallowed. There was nothing he could do ... but sell his soul and make a deal to save hers.

Zane broke the pen in his hand. If he could figure out where the monster took Rebecca, maybe he could rescue her.

And beat the evil spirit with his gun? A tear escaped his eye and he swiped at it. The last thing he needed was for anyone to see his pain. He groaned.

Zane really didn't care how he looked to others. He had gone far beyond that, into a world of self-loathing so dark he could never have imagined it existed, before he met Louis.

Never had he felt so hollow.

But he did have a plan. Once Rebecca was safe, he would kill himself. He would have to do it in such a way that it looked accidental so his family would get his life insurance, but one way or another, he had to go. He could never live with the knowledge that he had destroyed the lives of three innocent children.

A tune played on his cell phone sitting on his desk. He picked it up. The hourly picture of Rebecca was displayed. Underneath it Louis wrote: "I own you."

Yeah, yeah. Like he could forget.

The phone vibrated. The call came from an unknown source, but he knew who it would be.

"Constable Reynolds?" Louis's cold voice was unmistakable.

"Yes."

"I couldn't get the children." In a staccato, disjointed rhythm the spirit spoke to him. "The mother has a Viking ghost protecting her."

A Viking ghost? What the hell. If anyone had told him any of this supernatural crap existed a week ago, he would have thought they were crazy. Poltergeists, demonic spells, possession and now a Viking? The sound of his daughter screaming in pain in the background came through his phone.

"What do you want me to do?"

"Capture the children for me and take them to your house."

CHAPTER 13

TEA WITH AZALEA

When Abby entered the teahouse at noon the following day, Azalea stood beside the reservations desk. She acknowledged her with a nod. The natural light streaming through the large picture windows made the teahouse shine. Abby felt proud of her work. Without the night shadows and the laughter of the gambling ghosts the place seemed respectable. Then Lilith brushed the side of her leg and she reconsidered.

As if in answer, Azalea motioned her forward. "You need to speak to me?"

"Please. If you have a minute."

As the older woman nodded, the pile of white hair in a loose knot on the top of her hair shook. "This way."

Abby followed Azalea into Lilith's room and sat at the table the psychic pointed to. They were alone. The cat followed them in and jumped up on her window seat. She stretched in the sunlight and purred for a quick second, giving Abby the impression she considered herself the true hostess.

Azalea sat and waited.

Abby folded her hands in her lap. "I'm sorry to bother you." And she was sorry, very sorry. She needed this job more than she had ever needed a job. She didn't want to bother her boss. Ever. But Louis wanted her kids.

"I'm a good judge of character," Azalea said, peering over the tortoise shell glasses. "I know you wouldn't come to me without just cause. Is it the new detergent I bought? It is quite lemony." The agate pendant around her neck gleamed in the sunlight.

Soap? Seriously? "It's fine."

"Good. The last cleaner didn't like the stuff I had. Said it smelled too flowery. Then he quit." Her nose twitched. "You aren't quitting are you?"

"No. No, ma'am."

"What is it then?"

"I need your help." Couldn't the famed medium magically read her mind? Maybe this hocus-pocus stuff was all a joke after all.

"You didn't open the third door, did you?" Her eyes narrowed and burrowed into her.

Abby tilted her head and gave her a feeble smile.

Azalea frowned and shook her head. "I told you not to." She leaned back and crossed her arms across her chest. "So you have ghost trouble."

"Uh, no, not exactly."

"What then?" Azalea squinted.

"A poltergeist."

Azalea's spine stiffened and she sniffed the air. "In my town?"

Abby nodded. "I'm afraid so and he ..."

Azalea reached over and covered her hands with hers. Her stormy gray eyes glazed over to a muted seaweed color and she tilted her chin upwards as if the knowledge of the universe poured into her from the ceiling. "Yes, I see him now. You and Dodger and Louis. Wait … Dodger?"

"Yes."

"Damn that Louis."

"Yes." May all that is holy damn him.

Azalea made a low growling sound as she exhaled. "If I may, let me run your memory through my mind. It will be faster." She closed her eyes and mumbled five or six words. While her skin felt soft and her touch light, an unusual current flew between them as if they were connected.

Lilith, jumped down from her perch in the window seat and brushed against Abby's legs. First one way, and then the other, as if she were also conducting a psychic reading. Then she sat back on her feet under the table. Abby opened her mind to both of them as best she could.

A couple minutes later Azalea looked straight at Abby. "You are a strong woman. I commend you for standing up to a poltergeist, though Goddess knows, you had no choice. Your energy took him by surprise, but your words alone will not be enough to banish him the next time."

Ah, hell, that's what Eric had said. "What do you suggest?"

Lilith got up, ran back to her window seat and gave one long meow.

Azalea nodded at the cat and sighed. "I'll give you thirteen crystals to take home. Put them around the house at entrance points. They will yield some protection."

"Crystals." Shiny rocks. Seriously? How could a piece of rock stop that ghoul?

"And get a dog."

"A dog can't bite a black spirit."

"No, but it can warn you when a spirit approaches and that little bit of time could mean the difference between life and …" She hesitated a moment. "The alternatives."

Alternatives? Hell's bells she wasn't going to ask about that. "Okay, crystals and a dog. I'll beg, borrow or steal one if I have to. Anything else?" There had to be something else.

"Keep Dodger with you as much as you can. And …"

And? Abby waited for her to finish.

"Well, you're not going to like this, but the best way to deal with a poltergeist is to find out what made him go dark in the first place. It takes time to do this kind of research, but knowledge is the key in these matters. If you can find out what happened to him, you could ease his pain, which would diminish his anger and the demon's control over him."

"I can't Google that."

A thin, lopsided smile spread across her face and she snickered. "I have other sources." She sighed. "But I also have a business to run. I'll see what I can find out tonight."

"If you learn anything, please text me."

Azalea nodded, and as Abby rose, she added, "Ghosts don't make good boyfriends, by the way. Not for humans. I'd be careful with Dodger. I know he's sexy, but either one, or both of you, will get hurt if you let your relationship develop."

"He helped me last night."

"Oh, yes, he can be helpful, and he is mighty fine to look at, and charming in a Viking kind of way, but I'm sure you want more from a man than that."

Abby could feel heat rising n her cheeks. Of course she did. Any woman who looked at Dodger would, but that wasn't the sort of thing she talked about. Ever. "We're just friends."

"Uh-huh. That's fine love. Just don't go trying any of that G2H magic on him. I've lost too many good, ghost-friends that way. Spirits and humans should stick to their own kind, I say. I'm a traditionalist on that."

"G2H magic?"

"Ghost to human."

Abby blinked. Her world was becoming crazier by the minute. There was magic that could bring a ghost back to life? No. No, she wasn't going there. She had enough on her plate. "I really appreciate your help with Louis."

Azalea nodded.

"I hope you don't mind if I bring my kids to work with me tonight."

Azalea waved her hand in the air. "Of course not. I don't mind at all. The house will protect them."

Another chill crawled up Abby's spine and she found herself looking for the cat, as if she needed her approval as well. That settled it. The house and the damn cat were more than odd. The whole place reeked of supernatural power.

Lilith stretched and raised her back like a Halloween cat. If Abby was the kind of woman who scared easily, she would be terrified. But she wasn't, so she was just plain scared, chilled on the rocks, creeped out. Lilith lay back down again and winked. Winked? *No, I must be seeing things.*

Azalea touched her hand. "You'll get used to the house and to everyone who calls it home. It just takes time."

Abby sniffed and lifted her chin. "One more question."

"Shoot."

"Is your name really Azalea?" It had been bugging Abby, since she read the advertisement for her job on-line. Such an odd name.

The older woman's eyes twinkled. "Yes, my parents were hippies. My mother told me a beautiful azalea bush was in bloom outside our home the day I came into the world, so they named me after it."

"A bush."

She snickered. "A bush."

Abby could get used to that snicker. "I won't take any more of your time."

Azalea took both of her hands and squeezed them. "May the light of the world surround you and yours with love, hold you safe and protect you from all harm." Then she mumbled some foreign words and let go of Abby's hands, which stung from an ice-cold heat.

CHAPTER 14

LOVE IS LOVE

That night, as soon as Abby got the kids settled in a cozy corner of the reception area with blankets and pillows, she set about her chores. Within twenty minutes all three of them were fast asleep. Time passed slowly for her as every sound made her jump: the ticking of the clock in the reception room, the odd car that drove by and Lilith's snoring. But she persevered, determined to do a kick-ass job for Azalea who had to be the best boss ever. When she stopped for a cup of tea at midnight, the kettle was already boiling and Eric stood beside the stove.

Her heart beat kicked up. Amazing how a cold, dead spirit could create so much heat in a room. Having his perfect, warrior body so close, made her feel safe and hotter than hades. She pulled a hand over her hair smoothing it out as best she could. "I wondered where you had got to."

Did he know what he did to her? The confidence in his bad-boy smile said he did. "*Älsking*, if I was still alive I would pull you into my arms and hold you so tight I would feel your heart beat next to mine. I would feel the silkiness of your hair with my fingertips as I ran my hands through your beautiful mane. I would taste and taste again your full lips, until we both gasped for air."

She swallowed. "Eric," she said, noting a huskiness had seeped into her voice.

"I would trail sweet kisses up and down the length of you, along your luscious curves. And crevices. Aaah, your crevices. I would pull you tight against my manhood and feel you shudder with wanting."

"Oooh."

"What? I'm just getting started. Let me tell you more."

Her breath quickened. "Uh, I think that's enough for now." She fanned her face, which she guessed was bright red. "Tell me more about you."

Eric shrugged and poured the hot water into her tea pot. "What do you want to know?"

"How you died."

His image flickered a deeper silver, but, after a heartbeat, his square jaw firmed and he spoke. "As a boy I dreamed, like all Viking boys dream, of dying in battle and being sent to Valhalla."

"But you didn't die in battle."

"No, I died in an accident."

"What happened?"

"Did I tell you I imagine your lips taste like the juice of peaches ripened to perfection in the midday sun? Like aged wine made from the ripe grapes grown in the Cowichan valley. Like …"

"I never thought Vikings would be poetic." She wished she could elbow him or something. Yes, something.

"I am a Viking man, but like all men I have learned how to speak to women. And you have a *snygg rumpa.*"

Rumpa? Is he talking about my ass? "I get it. You've been sweet talking the ladies for over a century." *Hmm. Let's do the math. If he had one girl friend every fifty years that would be …*

He shook his head and his crystal blue eyes looked soft enough to break. "Do not diminish what we have, Abigail. For it is special, and we both know it."

"Just tell me how many?"

"How many times I would kiss you in an evening?"

She threw a cushion and it passed right through him, which made them both laugh. "No, how many women you've loved."

Eric looked around as if he had lost something. "In my bed, or in my heart?"

"Dodger."

He smirked. "Friends call me Dodger, but the name is a joke. I'd like you to call me Eric."

"Eric. Please, tell me what I want to know." His smile widened and he stepped closer. "It wouldn't matter how many women I have cared for in my mortal and ghostly lifetimes. The only thing that matters is you and me."

Sheesh, he could spin a line. "What am I to do with you?"

He sighed, but it being a ghostly sigh, the sound rumbled through the room as if it were a rock slide. "Oh, the dreams I have had of us together. Trust me, you would do many things."

Abby could not deny his effect on her. "Azalea mentioned a magic that would ..."

He held up his hand. "When your family is safe, we can talk of such things."

"So it exists?"

"Possibly." His eyes turned translucent.

Clump. Clump. Clump. Someone or something—she would keep her mind open to possibilities—was climbing the back staircase.

CHAPTER 15

AT THE BACK DOOR

Eric put his finger to his mouth and disappeared through the wall, leaving Abby staring at the back door. The footfalls were too loud to belong to a burglar. This person didn't care if he or she were heard. But why the back door? And why at midnight?

Knock. Knock. Knock.

Abby grabbed her cell phone out of her pocket in case she needed to dial for help and went to the door.

"Police," said a loud male voice from the other side.

Cops? She leaned against the door. Unfortunately, there wasn't a window for her to look through and check him out, or a security lens either. "I didn't call the police."

"There's been trouble in the neighborhood. I'm going door to door to check on people."

Trouble? Was the poltergeist bothering others? "What kind of trouble?"

"It would be easier to talk, if you opened the door."

"Tell me."

"Well, ma'am, it will make me sound like I'm crazy, but

we've had reports of a dark spirit roaming around. Looks like black mist."

Louis. People knew about Louis. The police knew! "Listen, I'm the night cleaner of the town's haunted teahouse. Talk about spirits doesn't sound weird to me."

"Then let me in." He knocked on the wood. "I'm sliding my business card under the door. My badge won't fit."

That made sense. His matter-of-fact demeanor sounded very-cop. She bent over and lifted his card off the floor. The RCMP logo on the top looked right. Below she read his name: Constable Zane Reynolds, Sunset Cove Detachment. The back was blank. It looked legit, but anyone with a printer could create it. "How do I know you're for real."

"I appreciate your hesitancy to open the door, ma'am, especially at this late hour. In fact, I applaud it. You can never be too careful these days. But I assure you, I am the police."

"Uh-huh." Where the hell was Eric?

"Okay, how about this. I'll stand back. You can crack the door open an inch and take a look at me. I'm standing here in my full uniform."

Man oh man, this guy was persuasive. But she was far too savvy to just open the door for a sweet-talking guy. Still, he only asked for an inch. She put her phone back in the pocket of her apron, grabbed a butcher knife from the counter and returned to the door. Holding the knife in the air with her right hand, she wedged her foot against the bottom to slow his entry. Carefully she cracked the door open a half inch and peered out.

The police officer stood there looking cookie-cutter perfect. Eric loomed behind him with his arms crossed over his chest. Clearly he wasn't impressed, but he wasn't interfering either. She opened the door fully.

"I haven't seen any dark spirits tonight," she said. And that was the truth.

He nodded. In the porch light it was hard to distinguish the color of his dark eyes, but he did look like a cop, not just because of his uniform, but because of his whole six-foot-tall and serious-as-stink manner. Not that she had anything against cops, especially good looking ones, just that they had, well, a common look about them.

"You sure?"

"Yeah."

"It's been spotted in the vicinity."

Fudge. "Like I said …"

"Mind if I look around?"

"Uh." She looked at Eric and he shook his head. "I don't think that's necessary."

Constable Zane pushed on the door and walked right past her as if she had agreed. "This won't take long."

Eric shimmered dark silver. They both followed the police officer into the reception area where the children slept.

"Kids, eh?"

"Yeah." She could explain why they were there, but she didn't.

"I got a daughter," he said. "Her name is Rebecca. She's two and sweeter than blackberry honey."

Okay, this guy could grow on her. Eric shimmered red as if he were ready to go poltergeist and his woodsy scent developed a burning ember tone. Had she missed something?

Zane stopped beside the baby. "And this one has to be the cutest."

She smiled. How could she not. Jane was gorgeous.

Zane picked her up. What the hell?

He nestled her in his arms. "Such a beautiful child, but that shouldn't surprise me. She has a beautiful mother."

Eric, now pure red, groaned and rolled his eyes. Zane

heard the rumbling, ghostly groan and looked around. "I thought you said there were no spirits."

"No, I said no *dark* spirits."

Zane's shoulders stiffened. He looked at the baby and then at Abby. His face contorted as if it had been placed in a vice and pinched. "I … I … can't do this."

Abby grabbed Jane from his arms. "What is *this*, exactly?"

"I can't steal your children."

An icy chill slid down her spine and she stepped back. "I'm not alone," she said.

The policeman looked around. "I don't see anyone."

Eric threw a tea cup and Zane, seeing it, ducked to avoid being hit.

"What the …"

"I told you, I'm not alone. I am protected."

Eric stood behind him. His eyes looked like orbs of fire.

Zane's eyes bulged and he took a big breath. "I'm so sorry. I shouldn't have come. It's against everything I believe in."

"Then why?" Eric's voice boomed through the room.

Zane turned to face the ghost, but she didn't think he could see him. "I said I was sorry. The … the …"

"Louis the poltergeist," said Abby.

"You kn … know about him?"

She nodded, keeping her calm, as if a discussion of the neighborhood evil spirit was an everyday thing. "We've met."

"I guess you have." He took off his hat and wiped the sweat off his brow. "He came to my house a week ago, in the middle of the night and he …" Zane wiped his brow again. "He took my Rebecca."

"Oh, sweet Jesus."

"She's the nicest kid you ever met. She lives in tutus and sings and dances and …" His voice broke. "She's so innocent."

"I'm sorry." Abby moved closer and rubbed his arm.

"Louis slid down Rebecca's mouth and in an instant she

lit up as if she were a Christmas light, and cursed like a sailor. She threw our dishes onto the floor. It was like watching the *Exorcist* movie. I didn't know what to do. My wife went hysterical and told me to make whatever deal I had to, to get her back."

"Deal?" Eric's voice thundered again. Boy he could be scary when he wanted to be.

"'Send you wife away,' Louis told me, 'and find me another child.'"

"Oh dear God, that must have been awful. He made you choose between giving up your child, or giving him someone else's."

"Exactly." Zane wiped his brow again. "So my wife went to her mother's and I drove around town trying to figure a way out of my pact with the devil."

"And Rebecca?"

His Adam's apple went up and then down. "She sits in a room somewhere, glowing and muttering curses. I know—at least I think I know— she's inside there somewhere, but what I see is not Rebecca. She's more Louis than human. He tells me if I don't find a suitable replacement, he will forever possess her and I will never see her again. He will roam the world inside her form doing whatever the hell poltergeists do."

"How awful."

He nodded. His eyes filled with tears. "So awful, I considered killing her myself. Maybe that would be the answer."

"Nooo." Eric again. "She is part his and if you took her mortal life, he would devour the last of her life energy into his evil spirit before she had a chance to die."

Zane closed his eyes. "I thought as much."

"There has to be something we can do." Abby's stomach twisted.

"I obeyed his orders and searched the town for children

who looked vulnerable. When I heard a widow had moved to town with three children, I checked you out. I'm sorry."

Abby folded her arms across her chest. She was well aware that she and the children would be considered vulnerable by many, because there was no man in the house, but the day Ben died, she vowed to herself to do everything she could to protect the kids. Hearing that she'd been profiled hit her hard. She had thought she put up a brave front, but how easily it had been seen through. Fudge. Heck. Double fudge.

"When Louis tried to take one of your children and you stopped him, he commanded me to take them. I thought I would start with the baby."

Tears rolled down Abby's face. "You can't have my baby. You can't have any of them."

"But Louis has my baby."

CHAPTER 16

GOOGLE-ON

Later that night, after Zane had left and she had finished cleaning the teahouse, Abby took her kids home. Two hours later she sat at her kitchen table staring at the laptop screen in front of her. She had tried every search term she could think of, but after an hour of research she had made no progress on finding out about the life of Louis Lament.

She dropped her head into her hands. What could she do? Azalea said she would find out what had happened to Louis, but she hadn't heard from her.

What next? She had to keep trying.

She typed into the Google search engine a new query. "Louis accident Vancouver Island." A bit of a stretch, but why not.

Boom. It worked. *The Orca News* had an article from 1950 related to her query. She clicked on it.

en-Year Old Boy Falls to his Death

After a three-day search, ten year old, Louis Lamentain was found dead in the forest behind the Orca Recreation Centre. According to Constable O'Rourke, communications officer for the local RCMP detachment, the boy's death may have been an accident. The rocky ledge beside the river is a treacherous place for children to play.

The boy died as a result of a severe blow to his head. While the immediate cause of the injury is clear, the investigation is not closed, as there have been reports the boy was the victim of bullying.

The question remains: Did he fall by accident from the rocky ledge or was he pushed?

His parents thanked the RCMP and the community for the search for their son.

bby checked through later copies of the newspaper. The following week there was a small article:

id Bullying Lead to Louiss's Death?

fter further investigation the police appear no closer to determining whether Louis Lamentain's death was accidental. If they know something, they aren't sharing it. A source reveals the teachers at the school wonder if it was a suicide. Several children bullied the boy because he was over-weight and small for his age. This is another lesson ...

*A*bby kept reading through following editions. Nothing. There just wasn't enough information about what happened to Louis, so she read all of the weekly editions around the date of his death.

The newspapers made Orca Beach sound like a quiet, peaceful seaside town. The headlines were usually about bake sales and pet by-laws. Human interest articles dominated, giving her the impression that it was a happy place to live.

But she'd seen enough of life to know that Norman Rockwell perfect towns don't really exist. People are people. There are good ones and there are the others. She kept reading.

Another picture of the town came through. It started with a small paragraph in one edition talking about complaints that a stranger had been seen lurking around the playground at the Orca Rec Centre. Then nothing for a few weeks. Then another paragraph. The stranger who wore a black jacket and ball cap was seen taking pictures of children. The police were unable to find him but said they would be patrolling the area. A week later Louis was found dead.

What did she have? A ten-year old kid, bullies and a lurking stranger. How had Louis died? She had to know.

She sent a text to Azalea. "Can you help me contact the poltergeist's parents or someone in his home town?" It was four in the morning, but she needed help.

Five minutes later Azalea responded. "Come to the teahouse. We will have a séance."

A séance? As in chatting with dead spirits? A week ago she didn't believe in ghosts and she certainly didn't believe in séances. Life was so much simpler then. Now she knew that not only did strange after-life things exist, she needed their help to save her children.

"On my way," she texted.

Eric had disappeared to talk with his friends about Louis. He said something about sliding into another dimension, so she couldn't ask him for help. She couldn't call Jillian or anyone else to babysit at this late hour either, so she packed up the kids—not an easy chore—and took them with her. Once at the teahouse she settled them into a corner of the receptions room.

~

Thirty minutes later Abby sat opposite Azalea in Lilith's room lit by a single candle in the middle of their table. The curtains were drawn and they were alone. The air smelled of a strong, earthy incense.

Abby swallowed. Part of her wanted to make fun of all of this spiritual stuff, but she couldn't. It was all too real.

"I have to warn you, Abby. The spirits you have met in the house are sociable and enjoy roaming our world. The ones we are about to call may not be. Prepare yourself. This could get ugly."

"Bring it on."

Azalea stared into the candle and chanted, words Abby didn't understand in a language she had never heard, an ancient tongue whose reverberations made her nerves dance. "I call the ancestors of Louis Lamentain." Azalea's other-worldly voice vibrated in the stillness of the night.

When Azalea raised her arms and looked upwards, the candle flickered, the door slammed shut, the window rattled and the air cooled

Abby's scalp tingled as if a horde of spiders crawled across it. The spirits had arrived. She gripped the edges of her chair.

A white shadow manifested behind Azalea. Abby's spine

straightened. She pointed.

"Are you related to Louis?" asked Azalea.

"Y … e…sss." The spirit's voice sounded distant and muffled.

"How did Louis die?"

Another white shadow shimmered. The two spirits floated on either side of Azalea.

Abby wanted to shout out to them, beg them for help, but she held her tongue.

Azalea spoke: "Louis has lost control. He hunts children to feed on. He has to be stopped. Tell us what happened to him, so that we can free his tortured soul. Together we can give him peace."

Abby tightened her grip.

"My son was a troubled boy." The man's voice came through Azalea's mouth. "Other children picked on him."

"Did one of them push him?" Abby couldn't stay quiet a moment longer.

"No." A woman's voice, this time. "I couldn't prove it, but I am sure, "—the air turned icy and the flame of the candle shot straight up— "it was the stranger."

"The stranger?"

"Louis was raped," the father said.

The mother sobbed.

"We made sure they didn't put that in the paper. But he was violated, repeatedly."

The sobs increased.

"It had to be that stranger. The other children wouldn't have done that."

"My son. My poor son." His mother's voice.

"Couldn't you do something?" Abby asked.

"I tried." It was the man's voice. "I hunted for the stranger, but he left town without a trace." His voice broke.

The mother cried. "I want Louis with me."

CHAPTER 17

SOME THINGS AREN'T DONE

"Enough," screeched Brunhilde, as she sucked Eric into her netherworld. "Enough, you idiot Viking."

"What now?" He landed on the rock floor of the cave.

"You are getting too involved in the lives of mortals."

"And a poltergeist."

"Well, him too. You don't need to be bothering with him either."

"He wants to suck the life out of innocent children."

She tilted her head and scowled as if to say, "so what," but she didn't say a word.

"I can't stand by and let that happen."

"What if I told you, you should. The affairs of mortals are not our concern. I need not tell you what happened to the last ghost of mine who got involved. The way she said "involved" made it sound like poison. "It didn't end well for anyone. Live humans don't understand us. They think we're cute, like puppies they can kennel when they get bored. But they don't really care for us."

"Abby's different."

"So you tell yourself. But my dear Viking, you're in for a big fall. She needs a real man, not one she can see through."

He wanted to say he was a real man, but he wasn't. He just wanted to be. He wanted to be a real man more than he had ever wanted to be a man, since his death. Because he wanted to be everything for Abby. So he grunted.

"In the name of Odin, don't grunt at me, barbarian."

"I am a royal Viking, not a barbarian and you're pissing me off."

"Hah!"

"I care for Abby. She cares for me. What could be more simple?"

"Let me make you a list."

"Nej."

"On the top I would put, "limp" as in limp."

"*Dra åt helvete.*"

"Next, I would write "ice cold," as in you're dead. Remember?"

"*Dra åt helvete.*"

"Third on the list, is—"

"I said, *dra åt helvete,* death bitch. Go to hell. I love her. I want to be with her."

"Ja, ja. So you say. But you're not thinking."

"You're so crude and cold. I don't need to hear your rants. I want to be with her. If she wants to spend time with me, what is the harm? We can be … companions."

"Just what every young widow needs." The old shrink circled him again and again with her menacing spirit and her obnoxious stench, an unholy union of rot and disinfectant. It was a good thing he hadn't digested food for hundreds of years, because one sniff of her would make him throw up.

Eric held himself still. "You're just jealous, old woman."

"Jealous?" She stopped and stood before him. "You think I'm jealous of a mortal?"

"You have not found anyone to console your restless spirit since your passing. Ja, you are jealous."

Her eyes blazed red for a second and then mellowed to swamp green. "We all find solace in our own ways. You seek a woman to love. Me ... well, let's just say it's more complicated. I do not seek redemption, or transcendence, or love. I am happy for the solace I get helping others."

Bullshit. But he wouldn't call her out on that. No one wants to hear that their life is pathetic. He really should pity her. She married an overbearing man and had a hard life and now she spent her time nagging ghosts. Surely there could be no—What did she call it? Solace?—in that. He folded his arms across his chest. "I am who I am. I know what I want. I want to be with Abby as long as she will have me."

"Why? Normally you spend your time flirting with women. Why attach yourself to this plain-looking widow?"

"Abby is not plain. Her strength shines through her. I love the person she is, strong and caring and pure. Do you know she sings her baby to sleep every night? She can't afford books, so she makes stories up for the other two. Every night they are tucked into bed with more care than any royal child."

"But she is mortal."

"Life and death are never fair."

"That we both know. So I have a plan for you."

Oh great. Words no ghost wants to hear from a death-shrink.

"I have been asking around on your behalf, and I may be able to secure you a place in the Christian heaven. You have adequate criteria.

"Heaven? With harps and angels?"

"Ja and when Abby dies she will find you."

"Heaven feels wrong to me. I am a Viking."

"Who missed Valhalla."

"Ja, but truly I am not ready to go anywhere. I will stay and haunt and there's nothing you can do about it."

Brunhilde growled low and deep. Her vibrations rattled through the cave bouncing back and forth between the walls, like foul smelling ping-pong balls. "Go then. Make a fool of yourself. But remember, when your heart breaks, I warned you, and I offered you a ticket to heaven."

CHAPTER 18

BATTLE ON

Abby climbed the ladder to put up the last Valentine heart. It had taken two days but when she got down and looked around, she felt her time had been well spent. The decorations transformed the haunted teahouse from scary to festive. Amazing what hearts could do. She stood and looked at them for a moment thinking back to all her Valentine celebrations. As a child her father would spoil her with treats, but her boyfriends had never been as thoughtful. Even Ben, as good a man as he was, had never been romantic about Valentine's Day. A shame really. It's the one day of the year when love is celebrated. Commercial crap aside, the real sentiment expressed on Valentine's Day could not be more perfect. She sighed. *True love, makes life worth living.*

Eric shimmered into view in front of her. He didn't need to say a word. The softness of his blue eyes told her how he felt. She swallowed. How could her feelings for him develop so quickly? She bit her lip. "Do you think Louis will appear tonight?"

He nodded. "He's hungry."

The woman screamed in the third room but it didn't rattle Abby. She checked her cell phone. 12:13, the same time as last night. Heck, she could start telling it was her break time by the woman's otherworldly shriek. Amazing how quickly one adapts to the strange. Ignoring it, she said, "I just wish we could trap him."

They moved to the kitchen and had tea. She told him about the séance and her research. He told her he had asked around, but hadn't come up with much. At two in the morning they bundled up the kids and headed for Abby's home.

Eric used his kinesthetic ability to float the two older children to their Mom's bed. Abby carried the baby and put her in the basket next to it.

After fussing over them for a few minutes, they went down to the living room and sat on the sofa together, close, but of course not touching.

Time passed slowly. Abby wanted to talk about something other than Louis. "Did you have a family?"

"Ja. I had four brothers and three sisters."

"And a wife?"

He hesitated before he spoke. "Ja, I was married at sixteen to strengthen the ties between my family and hers. She was nice."

"Nice? Just what I would want my husband to call me."

"We spent little time together. That was the way it was back then. I was always away fighting battles. If we had had more time, maybe we would have fallen in love."

"Children?"

He shook his head. "Two pregnancies, but neither came to term. That was not uncommon then, but I wondered."

"Wondered?"

"There was an herb women used when they didn't want to carry a baby to full term and I think she used it. She said she didn't mind losing the babies, that it was a sign she wasn't ready to be a mother."

Abby couldn't think of anything to say to that. How sad. A woman not wanting to have her husband's child.

He shrugged. "Life was not easy and she was very young. I don't think she felt herself ready for the responsibility."

"But you love children."

"Ja."

"Did she know that?"

He shrugged and looked towards the door, but there were no sounds.

"If I was her I would have had your babies. Lots of them."

"Ja. I know you would."

He blew air towards her so the hair swished away from her face. "I planned to give her more attention, but we never had time. I don't blame her. I don't linger in the past."

"I'm sorry."

His eyes softened. "It makes our time together sweeter."

What could she say to that. "There is nothing more important to me than my children. I wish you could have had that."

"I have this moment with you. That is all any of us have."

"So you like hanging out with me because I have kids?"

"Nej, I like hanging out with you because you are you."

Pluto growled, low and deep. The air temperature plummeted. Black mist seeped under the front door.

Louis had arrived.

Eric stood and motioned for her to stay put. Like hell.

The damp, dark cloud gathered before them and manifested into the form of a boy.

Abby's heart jumped into her throat.

∽

"*E*nough poltergeist." Eric faced Louis. This had to stop.

It was a final battle. Only one of them would survive in this dimension. If Louis won, Eric would meet the ultimate death. One with no afterlife. Eternal darkness within and without, a darkness that pressed in until there was nothing but darkness. All essence would be vanquished, leaving a spiritual, black hole. If Eric won, Louis would join his mother in heaven. It didn't seem fair, but death never was. This was what Eric had learned from his friends that he didn't share with Abby. He was risking everything for her.

Louis expanded until his power took up a quarter of the room, a cloud of swirling black energy, kinetically whirling all objects in its path into a cyclone. Eric watched. There had to be a way to stop his insanity.

Louis laughed, a maniacal sound that would churn the gut of a mortal Viking, but made Eric madder. The poltergeist threatened the life of the woman he loved and her children. He had never had children, so they would become his if he had his way. He could not have any of them harmed.

"Enough." Eric pulled a sword from the harness on his back, wishing the spirit had some flesh he could slice and dice.

"No Viking. It will not be enough until I have at least one child."

"Nej."

"Oh yes. You can't stop me. I will take one child and then another. In fact, I think I'll take the woman while I'm at it, just to spite you."

Eric's jaw clenched. "How inclusive."

"I've never been inside a woman before. In her body I'll have fun with the men in town. With those full breasts.

Mmm. I wonder how many will want to hold them. And then there's her ass ..."

Eric had been a distinguished warrior, trained to still his anger for battle. He tried as hard as he could to hold his temper, but it wasn't working. He wanted to crack a skull or two and unfortunately Louis had none. There had to be a way to end this spirit-asshole.

Abby got up from the couch and moved beside him. For the love of Odin, what was the woman thinking?

"Louis," she said.

The poltergeist moved towards her.

"Oh settle down, I'm not afraid of you."

Eric couldn't believe his ears. Had the woman no sense? She should be terrified. He had more power than all of the gambling ghosts put together.

"You're just a big baby," she said to the evil spirit, ignoring Eric's stare.

Louis stopped in front of her.

"You are a 'little man.' That is what your mother calls you. I talked with her. She cried and cried. She misses you. She wants you to be with her. It's time for you to join her."

The spirit force drained from his human form and congealed into a puddle on the floor. "Momma?"

Eric moved towards him. Louis's face could be seen in the puddle.

"Yes, your mother misses you," said Abby

"Momma?"

"She remembers rocking you in her arms. She remembers your sweet laughter. She remembers ..."

"Stop." Louis lifted an arm out of the puddle. "Please stop."

"She remembers the good in you Louis. She can't change anything about your horrific death, though she wishes she could. But she can be with you now."

Oh Valhalla. Like that's going to work on a badass.

"I am no longer her child." Louis's voice took an ugly tone.

"You are, and always will be, her baby." The softness of Abby's voice melted Eric's heart. It was the voice of a mother: simple, calm and filled with an eternal truth about the bonds that unite us all. Even though they cut the cord between a mother and child at birth, the bond never dies.

"I can't go back. I can never go back."

"That's where you're wrong," Eric said. "The universe and all its realms are greater and more pliable than your mind could ever imagine. You know in your heart what the unifying force is. You just have to let it in."

The puddle turned a translucent blue, like water on a sunny, spring morning. It swallowed up what was left of his face.

"Louis, your mother wants you." Abby looked down at what was left of him. "Go to her Louis. Prove once and for all that you are the little man she believes in."

"But…"

"But what Louis?"

"I'm not finished here."

Silence fell for a moment and Eric worried that they had lost him.

His puddle became bluer and the smell of an ocean breeze hit the air. "My death wasn't fair."

"No," said Abby, "it wasn't. And I'm sorry for that. Truly sorry. But hurting others, will not right that. The evil man who raped and killed you is dead. Long dead."

"I suffered. Others should suffer."

"Does it make you feel any better?" said Eric. If someone had told him he would be counselling a poltergeist to the far side, he whould have told them they were crazy. Yet here he was doing just that. Abby was good for him. It seemed to be working. He would see his enemy die without any blood being shed. A true first for him.

"I see a light." Louis's puddle glowed.

"Be a man. Let it in." Eric said.

Louis sighed.

CHAPTER 19

VALHALLA

As the puddle evaporated into tiny light bubbles, the room warmed. Eric started towards Abby, but Brunhilde appeared between them and an instant later he found himself once again in her cold, damp chambers between the realms.

"Let me go," he said.

"You vanquished a poltergeist."

She looked softer around the edges than usual, but he didn't care about that. All he cared about was being with Abby. "Let me go."

"I have heard from the gods, from Odin himself, in fact.

"I don't give a shit. Let me go."

"You have done good in the world, when you were alive and afterwards and now you have saved a family."

He grumbled.

"You are a soul of the light."

He grumbled louder. Loud enough that his voice rumbled through the cave.

"Odin says after this battle you have proved yourself worthy of Valhalla. He is making an exception for you, giving you a special entry permit. You will rise in your beloved Valhalla as a wounded warrior, victorious in battle."

"Nej."

"What?"

"Nej."

"Have you lost your mind? Odin. *The* Odin, has given you the green Viking light."

"I don't care. I don't want to be in Valhalla."

"There are beautiful, Swedish maidens waiting to take care of all of your needs."

He narrowed his eyes. "I do not want a bevy of maidens. I want …"

"Abb,." Brunhilde finished his sentence. He couldn't be sure, but he could swear her hard eyes softened in that moment.

An instant later he was back with Abby.

CHAPTER 20

SWEET ENDINGS

Eric sighed as he stood as close to Abby as he could. Inhaling her womanly scent made his spirit stir. "Death doesn't get any better than this."

Abby laughed.

"Tell me, äskling, how do you feel about being haunted by a Viking?"

Her eyes locked with his. "Bring it on."

How many human women would want to be haunted by any man, let alone one as old and crusty as him? He wished he had something special to give her. Then he got an idea. "Tell me, Abby, about your writing."

"Well, I write mysteries"

"Is it the writing you like or the mystery?"

She blinked. "Both, I guess. Why?"

"I'd like to be your partner."

"You're a ghost."

"I know that."

"A dead ghost."

"Got that."

She smirked. "What are you suggesting?"

Eric floated back and forth across the room. "Azalea has an attic."

Abby stared at him as if he had lost his mind.

"I could persuade her to let us use it. The ceiling is high and the light from the old lamps has a warm, golden quality. The front window overlooks the cove, and through the back window you can see her garden."

"That sounds nice. I guess. But what do we need an attic for?"

"The heat in the house rises, so it is always warm up there. You wouldn't need to pay much for heat."

"Uh-huh."

"And the teahouse has an excellent night cleaner."

"You got that right."

"The area is respectable enough and everyone in town knows where the house is, so when they ask where your office is and you tell them, the teahouse, they'll know where to find you."

"My office?"

"Every respectable detective has an office. Even I know that."

Abby walked over to her sofa and plunked herself down. She rubbed her forehead. "I'm not a detective. I'm a wannabe writer."

"You figured out how to take care of Louis. I would call that fine sleuthing. You understand the Google."

"Uh-huh. And what would you do?"

He gave her his most devilish smile. "I'm your muscle."

~

*A*bby ran a hand through her hair. It had to be the craziest idea she had ever heard of —opening a detective agency with a ghost—but something about it, felt absolutely right. Just being with Eric felt right. Talk about crazy times. Her life had taken a turn away from normal to something much better, filled with magic and love. Did she just think the love word? Oh heck. It must be because of all the excitement. No one falls in love this quickly.

"I can't imagine there are many mysteries in our small town," she said, trying to keep her mind on practical things.

"You won't know unless you ask." His deep voice held enough confidence for the two of them. Sweet Jesus she … cared … for this guy. He made her feel as if the impossible task of starting a business was possible. Her shoulders dropped an inch. Maybe she didn't have to struggle to feed her children. If she could pull off a day job on top of a night job, maybe … just maybe she could make a decent living.

"But I don't know how much to charge people. Or how to advertise. Or …"

"All in good time. First we talk to Azalea. She's good at business. I'm guessing she'll rent you the attic for free at first, and she'll help you with the paper stuff. Having a good business upstairs will help her business. You two work well together."

Abby thought about the strange woman with the white hair piled on top of her head. They had developed an unusual bond.

She shook her head. "Wait, just one moment. About the muscle."

He laughed. "My äskling, you'd be surprised what I can do. You must know, I would do anything to protect you. I would move heaven and earth if you asked me."

She had Googled äskling and found out it meant darling, and the way he said it with his deep gravelly voice made her knees wobble. Torn between trying to drown the idea in her mind with skepticism and her heart leaping for joy at the thought of pursuing a dream she never dared admit to, she ran her hand through her hair. "The Ghost and the Widow Inc?"

Eric tilted his head. "How about Valhalla Investigations? Working with Abby would be his Valhalla, his heaven.

"Tag line: I'll get your man."

"Heh, I'm your man." The timbre of his voice deepened. "Always and forever. You don't need any other."

"Uh-huh" She grinned as if she mocked him, but her insides quivered. As it … as if it were the truth.

"If that's okay with you."

"We'll see," she said, but her heart already knew.

CHAPTER 21

VALENTINE'S DAY

The next morning Abby woke up to Jonathan and Jinx jumping on her bed. The mattress went up and down with their enthusiasm as if it were a trampoline. "Mommy, Mommy."

"What?" She cracked an eye and sniffed. Was that coffee she smelled?

"Look. Look what we found in our beds this morning," said Jinx holding up her treasure.

Abby cracked the other eye. They both held chocolate Valentine hearts the size of their little hands.

"Oh my goodness." Out of the corner of her eye she saw a vase filled with long-stemmed roses on her bedside table and a box of chocolates with a red ribbon wrapped around it.

The Viking was more than muscle.

Zane with the help of a police dog found Rebecca healthy, but a wee bit confused. She said she'd had a bad dream. Her mom came home and their family is happy.

Abby and Eric started Valhalla Investigations in the attic of the haunted teahouse. They haven't had any cases yet, but they talk a lot about finding the ancient magic that would breathe life into his ghostly specter. We may need to check in on them later.

AFTERWORD

Abby and Eric's story continues in the series *A Ghost & Abby*. Here is the first chapter in the first book, *Midnight Magic*.

I'll Always Remember my First

I'm the night janitor in a haunted teahouse, in the small, Pacific Northwest town of Sunset Cove, where things happen no one talks about. Ever. You'd think that would be enough weirdness for one person in a lifetime, but not for me. I've started a business on the side, to sort and sanitize supernatural drama. That is to say, I am the community's first private detective. My name is Abby Jenkins.

I've studied sleuthing for years, reading every Nancy Drew, Agatha Christie and Charlaine Harris book in the public library. I rock at jigsaw puzzles. I'm naturally nosy. And my whopper-credential is that I know all the usual suspects in town, both of the human and supernatural kind. Of course we get visitors, but that's beside the point. I figure I can solve a local whodunit with the best of them, especially if there's a butler involved. What could possibly go wrong?

Although my jobs may sound unusual, I'm not a freak. I look like a regular thirty-two-year-old mom, the kind you see at the grocery store herding her three young children through the shopping aisles. My blond hair lives in a creative ponytail and my thrift-store clothes are stained with life. I can't remember the last time I put on makeup. I avoid mirrors, not because I'm a vampire, but because they make me cranky. You could easily pass me by, and profile me as a normal, single-mom-next-door, a minion in the landscape of America. But I'm not. Unusual things happen to me.

It's as if I have a sticker on my forehead, reading: "Send me your ghosts, poltergeists and living dead, and see what happens." Some people call me, "*that* widow," others, "the janitor in *that* place," and now some call me, "the private dick without a dick," but I refuse to be defined. I am simply Abby.

Let me tell you about my first case. Trust me, I'll always remember my first.

***

At 2 p.m. on a stormy day suitable for ducks, I sat at my desk across from my first client in the attic of the Sunset Cove Teahouse, a Victorian gingerbread home with a wicked reputation for things that go bump in the night. The palms of my hands itched. I had never expected to live out my dream of being a detective, and I wasn't sure I could pull it off.

I pushed a box of tissues across the desk towards the woman, hoping to stop her tears. She had cried since she entered my office, four minutes ago. I didn't know her name or why she arrived at my doorstep. She walked in and sat down. Her fancy scent made my nose twitch.

I drummed the old, oak desk with my fingers and watched the seconds tick by slowly on the antique clock hanging askew on the opposite wall. My stomach twisted. This was not what I expected for my first day. I figured I would be looking for lost cats, wandering spouses or, at worst, lost souls. I had not anticipated tears.

My visitor was a noisy, theatrical crier, all sniffles and broken sighs. Her face flushed crimson and perspiration beaded her forehead, all signs she was definitely a live human. I checked the clock. Six minutes had passed.

I didn't recognize her, so she had to be new to town. Fine lines radiated from her eyes. I pegged her to be a well-preserved forty-five. Her trembling right hand, holding a tissue to her nose, had a salon manicure. An expensive charm bracelet dangled on her wrist. Her left hand, resting on her lap, had a ring with enough diamonds to sink a casket. My fine sleuthing abilities surmised she could afford me.

"It's haunted," she blurted out. She blew her nose loudly and commenced crying again.

"I know," I said. Of course I knew. Everyone knew. The Sunset Cove Teahouse was haunted and an interesting gang of ghosts called it home. It was only quiet at that moment because they played elsewhere during the day. All I could hear in the house was the sound of people—of the breathing variety—coming and going from Azalea's teahouse on the main floor, looking to find good fortune in their tea leaves. Azalea, the owner of the house was, among other things, a talented tea-leaf reader. The house belonged in a catalogue for the Best Haunted Businesses.

Trying to retain my cool PI persona I looked out my window. I could see most of Sunset Cove, a small inlet with a few boats, and a sleepy town nestled in a cozy semicircle around it. My window box overflowed with purple petunias, yellow pansies and midnight-blue lobelia. The sweet scent of the flowers almost masked the smell of the supernatural. I breathed in my Norman Rockwell moment, determined to wait out the woman's tears.

They continued.

I squirmed in my seat, and I was not a squirmer by nature. Her problem had to be big, but that didn't cut it with me. Label me a thrift-store snob if you like, but she looked way too comfortable to have any real issues, like starvation or marginalization. Or how about cultural genocide? Maybe her poodle got a bad haircut.

Most people dress casually in our sea-side town of five thousand people. For women, yoga pants or leggings with cool footwear covers you anywhere at any time, but she wore a pair of navy-blue dress pants, a white silk blouse and a well-cut blazer; an impressive power outfit, designed to take control of any situation. Her straight, platinum-blond, shoulder-length hair had enough highlights for a fashion cover. She wore black-leather stilettos with red soles that would cost more than six months of my part-time janitor's salary. What could this woman possibly know about trouble?

She sniffed loudly.

"Would you like a cup of coffee?" I said.

She shook her head. "I need help." She broke into another elongated sob.

The ticking of the clock echoed in the room. What did one do with a whimpering woman? I took a deep breath and decided to wait out her emotional episode. After all, doesn't everyone need a good cry every now and then?

I am an expert on the power of crying. Two and a half years ago my husband died of cancer, leaving me with three children to raise, all under the age of six. Losing my high-school sweetheart broke my heart. Having to raise our kids on my own almost broke my backbone. I cried a lot as I pulled my life together, but I did it. I built a new life for myself.

The icing on this new life was to be this supernatural-PI

gig, but it wasn't looking too sweet at this moment. Why had I ever thought taking on other people's problems would be fun? In one word, Eric. That's why. My boyfriend Eric talked me into the mystery business. "Become a detective," he said. "You love to solve mysteries," he said. "You're a natural," he said. "And I'll help," he said.

Yeah right. At this moment, as I faced the whimper-queen, I felt like a real natural: a natural idiot. And he wasn't here.

I handed her another tissue. "My name is Abby and I want to help you." This was the third time I had said that, but this time she stirred.

Sitting back in her chair she made eye contact. Behind the tears, the hardness of her baby-blues jolted me for a second. This was no ordinary wilting woman.

"Charisma Dubois," she said with a slight French accent that purred.

I nodded.

"I have a problem I'm told only you can help me with."

Me? Did she want advice on breast feeding? How about potty training? I did have some awesome coping tips for late-night diarrhea. Nope, I guessed none of the above by the look of her. "Go on," I said.

"I have inherited a property."

"That's nice," I said with trepidation, because something in her tone was off.

"Oh, I don't care about the property. I will sell it after …"

"After?"

"After I find the treasure."

Of course, there would be property and treasure. "Treasure?"

"My great-grandmother Louise Dubois was a bit odd."

"I see," I said, though I didn't see at all.

"She didn't believe in banks and kept all her assets in diamonds."

"And the diamonds are in the house."

"Yes. Maybe. I'm not sure. I'm not sure at all, actually." She stopped to sob. "According to my uncle's will," she continued, "I have been left my great-grandmother's manor. No one has ever found her diamond stash and I believe it's there."

"Did anyone else inherit?" I didn't want to get in the middle of a family feud. I'd seen too many murder mysteries about them.

"No. I'm the only living relative, and my uncle bequeathed me the house and all its contents."

"Okay. So you want me to clean it so you can find the stash?" It was a Lysol job after all. Right up my alley.

The woman's eyes shot wide. "Heavens, no."

"Then what do you want me to do?"

Her spine stiffened as she raised her pointed chin. "I want you to find my diamonds."

"Why don't you go into the house and look?"

"I tried that." Staring at a spot above my head as if the answer were there, she wiped gently at her nose. "I was told you understand abnormal things, things beyond the normal, supernatural events and such."

"Are you saying the house is haunted?"

"It would seem so. Yes." The color in her red face drained to a sage-green hue. Now the hysterical crying made sense. Encounters with the dead unravel the best of us.

My squirmy butt froze. "Okay, let me get this straight. You want me to go with you to a haunted house and look for diamonds."

"Yes," she said with glee. "But not with me, Ms. Jenkins. No, no, I don't want to go back there. I'm from Montreal. I'll pay you to find the treasure for me. I'll pay you well."

"Uh-huh." Clearly something in the house had scared the

bejesus out of Ms. Dubois. If I was a sane person I would've turned her down right then and there, especially given my experience with a poltergeist, but the scent of mystery pulled on my natural and too abundant curiosity. Not to mention the thought of having extra money in my pocket. I rubbed my chin.

"I'll pay you double your normal fee."

I pushed a contract her way. "I'll start with a two-hundred-dollar retaining fee, and I'll charge you by the hour. If you write down the address I'll get started tomorrow." Surely Eric would turn up by then and we could go together during the day when most ghosts are busy in other dimensions. I gave her a professional smile and myself a mental thumbs-up.

"I want you to start today."

I nodded. Of course, Ms. Power Suit would demand more than I was willing to give.

After she filled out the contract and handed me five-hundred dollars in cash, she wrote down the address, which I read out loud: "Graystone Manor, 333 Witch's Peak Road."

"It's five miles north of town, up a windy road, but not hard to find," she said. Her eyes narrowed to pinpricks. "I will pay you double your regular fee for every hour you look for the treasure and an extra finder's fee when you retrieve the stash." She hesitated a moment. "Say ten thousand dollars."

Ten thousand? *Oh my word!* My heart raced. There were so many things I could do with that kind of money, starting with finding a place to live without a leaky roof.

I bit my lip. I needed to concentrate on things at hand. Witch's Peak? I didn't know there was such a road. For that matter, I didn't know there was another haunted house in town. I had so much to learn.

"The sooner you start the better," she said as she pulled a set of keys out of her purse and handed them to me.

I stood to shake her hand and wondered.

Better? Is that better for me? Better for her? Or better for the ghosts?

Midnight Magic is available on Amazon

ACKNOWLEDGMENTS

Thanks go to my team:

Cover Designer: Steven Novak

Editor: Dr. Philip Newey

Beta Readers: Gina Smith and Sandra Singleton. I could never do this without you ladies.

and PJ, my husband who always supports me even though romance on paper is not his thing.

ABOUT THE AUTHOR

Reports of Jo-Ann Carson's death on a Gulf Island are greatly exaggerated or, at the very least, premature. An award-winning fiction and non-fiction author, blogger and podcaster, Jo-Ann loves to tinker with words. Her latest two series the **Ghost & Abby Mysteries** and the **Gambling Ghosts** feature eccentric characters, such as a Viking ghost with existential issues, a broken-hearted Highlander and a Casanova-man-witch. At the center of each tale is a strong woman trying to make sense of life and love.

A firm believer in the magic of our everyday lives, Jo-Ann loves watching sunrises, and walking the beaches near her home in the Pacific Northwest. You can find her at her author website: http://www.jo-anncarson.com/.

Writing as Doomsday Carson

Bete Noire